The
Twin Flame
Rebellion

Also by Michelle Gordon:

Earth Angel Series:
The Earth Angel Training Academy
The Earth Angel Awakening
The Other Side
The Twin Flame Reunion
The Twin Flame Retreat
The Twin Flame Resurrection
The Twin Flame Reality
The Twin Flame Rebellion

Visionary Collection:
Heaven Dot Com
The Doorway to PAM
The Elphite
I'm Here

The Twin Flame Rebellion

Michelle Gordon

The Amethyst Angel

First published in Great Britain in 2017 by The Amethyst Angel

Copyright © 2017 by Michelle Gordon
Cover Design by madappledesigns, The Amethyst Angel &
Soulscape Design

ISBN: 978-1-912257-13-3

The moral right of the author has been asserted.

First Edition

Gratitude

I think one of the hardest parts about publishing a book is knowing how to adequately thank all the amazing people who were a part of the journey. The ones who fed me, or housed me, or cheered me on, or supported me, or kicked my ass right out of procrastination.

Without them, this book wouldn't be in your hands right now, entertaining you, making you laugh, or cry, or get angry. It would still be a mess of scribbles on a page, or even just a random idea in the ether, undefined and blurry.

I hope all the people I love know just how much I appreciate their love and support, but just in case they need a reminder, I will thank them again here.

Thank you, Mamma, you are my biggest fan and supporter and I love you so much. Without your encouragement to follow my heart and do what I love, I would never have been able to become a writer. I love you forever.

Liz Lockwood, what can I say? You are my sanity in the craziness, you are my best friend, you are a rocking editor, and you never tell me to be sensible or normal. I love you, Angel, and I'm so proud of you for writing your first book, it's truly beautiful. Liz's book is called Little Something, I really recommend it.

Lizzie, my wonderful big sister, why do you put up with me? I know I drive you totally crazy, but I love you so much for supporting me and my mad dreams.

Tiffany, you are my productivity inspiration! I seriously can't wait to read your book. Get it written! Thank you for becoming a Patreon too, you are amazing.

Thank you, Fyn Day, for providing the sunny rooftop on which most of this book was written, and for making lovely food and for all the celebratory sorbets!

Mr Bee, oh you do make me laugh, I'm so glad our paths crossed and I hope that you approve of your namesake in the book!

Laurie Huston, you beautiful Old Soul, thank you for your hospitality and friendship, and for telling everyone you know about this series. I hope you like your character ;)

Thank you to my New York buddies Mandy Reid and Jonathan Berkowitz, for inspiring characters in the story.

Robert Tremblay, you are the most inspiring man I have ever met. No matter what life throws at you, you just keep going, regardless. You are amazing. Thank you for your hospitality and your friendship, and for inspiring parts of this book. Reader, please go and buy Robert's book, it's called Twenty Seconds and is available on Amazon.

Thank you, Margaux Joy Denador, your love of this series is making some serious magic happen, and I cannot thank you enough! Love to your husband, Dudley and brother, Duane, who love the books thanks to your recommendation!

Lovely Nicole Brookdale, I love our chats and your continued support and encouragement, I look forward to meeting you in person one day soon.

Beautiful Faerie Niki, I have no idea how you do what you do, but you're so very inspiring! If you could bottle your Faerie power I would definitely buy some! Love you. x

Thank you, Lu and Andrew, for putting me back together again when I started to fall apart! You're both awesome.

Thank you for your love and support, my beautiful Angel sister Kelly. You've always believed in me so much, and I love you.

Thank you, Helen, for always being my number one fan, and for buying every book. Much love and hugs to you.

Thank you, Aitreya of Spirits Child, for your hospitality and for allowing me to mention your beautiful establishment in the story.

Thank you, lovely Patreon patrons, for your continued support. You are making this book possible! Thank you, Kariel Tejai, Vikki Elizabeth Finlay, Sandy Townsend, Ana Leon, Tiffany Hathorn, Trisha & Bruce Barnes and Sandra Lipowski.

Jon, you are such a beautiful soul, my only wish is for you to see yourself as I see you. You have brought me so much magic and laughter and love, there really are no words that can properly express how grateful I am to have you in my life. I love you.

This book is for my spirit sister,
Starlight, aka Sarah Rebecca Vine.
(The most rebellious Earth Angel I know.)

And it's for Robert Tremblay,
a man who thrives against all odds.

Chapter One

"What is this?"

Greg looked up at Violet from where he was cutting up kindling outside the back door. His gaze clocked the letter in her hand and his shoulders dropped.

"Oh, um, it came the other day."

"Why didn't you tell me?" She was trying to keep the tone of disappointment out of her voice, but was afraid it had managed to seep in anyway.

Greg shook his head. "I was dealing with it. I didn't want you to worry."

Violet sighed. "I thought we agreed that we would always be totally transparent with each other, that we wouldn't ever keep secrets."

Greg lay the axe down on the chopping block and walked over to Violet. She looked up at him, and smiled at the sad, puppy dog look on his face. "I'm sorry," he said. "I just wanted to be able to sort it out myself."

"I know," she said softly, reaching out and pulling him into her arms. "But we're a team, we do this together, okay?"

She felt him nod against her shoulder as he held her tightly. She breathed in his woodsy scent and thanked the Universe yet again for bringing her best friend and Twin Flame to her, and for every moment they had spent together so far.

She pulled back a little and kissed him deeply on the lips.

He responded and she felt her earlier tension melt away.

"I love you," she whispered. "I will organise another retreat. If I get the details online today, I'm sure we can get enough bookings to cover this bill."

"But you're already doing so much, you can't do another retreat as well."

Violet smiled. "Of course I can. I can do anything when I set my mind to it." She kissed him again then released him and went back inside. Once she stepped into the house, her smile disappeared and she sighed softly to herself. She had just preached the importance of transparency and honesty, and then lied. She was too tired to do another retreat, but how else would they pay the bill for the recent repairs they'd had done?

Violet put the kettle on and made herself a cup of tea, then went to her office. She fired up her laptop and put the bill in the in-tray to be sorted. She did some quick calculations, and worked out how long and how big the retreat would need to be to cover the bill.

It pained her that she had to think of retreats in that way. She wished she could run them for the sole purpose of helping others and Awakening the world, but it seemed like it always came down to money. And for some reason, no matter how hard she and Greg worked, it just wasn't enough. They always had bills coming in that cleared them out again.

Violet frowned. She had noticed recently that the issue of abundance was a big thing amongst her friends, too.

Did Earth Angels have a problem with manifesting and receiving?

Instead of creating the new advert for the retreat, Violet visited some pages and forums that many Earth Angels frequented, and read through the posts. After an hour, she remembered to drink her tea, which was now stone cold.

She leaned back in her chair, her mind whirring. It appeared that a large number of Earth Angels were experiencing lack and scarcity.

But why? They were beings from realms and planets where scarcity did not exist. They knew they were Earth Angels, they knew they were here for the soul purpose of Awakening humanity, and they knew how to manifest.

So why were they having so much trouble with money and finances?

Violet finished the rest of her cold tea, musing over the question. Even she was struggling, in spite of everything she knew about her previous existence on the Other Side, and in spite of knowing that the Universe was abundant and lack was a state of mind.

Violet checked her calendar and saw that it was a new moon that evening. Time to call upon her Spiritual Sisters for a meeting.

She typed a quick message and sent it, then refocused on creating the advert for the new retreat.

* * *

"What are you watching?"

Mica looked up from where he sat on the pebbly shore, to see Emerald approaching him. Her wings were beating powerfully yet silently, and they lowered her down gently to where she came to rest beside him.

"Velvet and Laguz. It's been a while since I last checked in on them, I was curious to see how they were getting on."

Emerald sat down on the pebbles, shifting about until she was comfortable. She looked down at the glassy surface of the lake. "And how are our beautiful Old Souls doing?"

Mica looked at his Flame and frowned. "Not great, actually. They're struggling financially, and I can see that Laguz's light is dimming under the weight of the responsibility to keep the Twin Flame Retreat going. I feel a little bad that I left the Retreat to them, that I pretty much forced them to take it on, and didn't even ask them if it was what they wanted. I just couldn't bear the thought of the Retreat not continuing when so many Flames needed it. And when it was something that you and I built together."

Emerald took his hand. "I can understand that, and I don't think they saw it as a burden. But I can see that perhaps they feel they must continue to run it, to honour us, and that if they felt they needed to do something else, they might not choose that path."

Mica nodded, and watched Velvet as she hung up some washing on the line in the garden. "Have we messed with their Free Will? And in doing so, have we messed with the bigger picture?"

Emerald thought about it for a moment. "It's an interesting question. I don't know if anyone has even seen the bigger picture since Starlight left for Earth. I wonder how different it is to the original timeline, when Velvet went home to the stars."

"Is there anyone here we can ask? Pallas? Gold?"

"I'm not sure they have access to it. Why don't we contact Starlight? Ask her through her dreams to show us. After all, she is the Angel of Destiny, if anyone would know, it would be her."

Mica got to his feet and held out his hand to help Emerald up too.

"Let's do it."

"Right now?"

Mica smiled. "Now is all there is."

*   *   *

"I appreciate you all coming at such short notice, but I saw that it was a new moon tonight and I wanted to take advantage of that."

Violet looked around the room at her Sisters and could see they were intrigued.

"It's come into my awareness that many Earth Angels seem to be having issues with abundance, and seem to be stuck in places of lack and scarcity. I know that I am certainly having these issues currently, and so I thought I would call upon you all to see if we could come up with some ideas on how to change or improve this. I don't believe for a second that we Earth Angels are meant to live in lack, or that we're meant to struggle. I think that when we have a solid, stable foundation, we are much more likely to be able to fulfil our missions on this planet."

~ 4 ~

"I completely agree," Julie said. "I know that I have been struggling with the same issues, and I also know that I really don't want my kids to grow up in lack and scarcity because it will just perpetuate through to the next generation."

Lisa nodded. "So many of my friends are going through the same issues, and they're struggling to keep going. Many of them have businesses in holistic therapies, and they're all so giving and generous with their time, energy and money, but when it comes to receiving, they seem to have a great deal of difficulty with it."

There were a few moments of quiet as the women contemplated the issue, and sipped their hot drinks. Violet grabbed another biscuit and nibbled on it.

"This might be completely unrelated, and if so, I apologise, but I'm going to throw it out there," Beatrice said.

Violet nodded. "Please do," she said.

"It occurred to me that a lot of this has to do with focus, acceptance, and a strong motivation." Beatrice sipped her coffee before continuing. "When our focus is on what we want, but do not have, we just keep experiencing the wanting of it, because we are coming from a place of lack. When our focus is on something we have, then we get more of that, because we are coming from a place of abundance." Getting into the stride of her ideas, Beatrice stood up and started wandering around the room. "Acceptance is about loving and appreciating everything exactly as it is, and not being at war with what is. As soon as you resist something and begin a war, then you will always be fighting, holding on to what you need to let go of, and blocking what is waiting to come to you."

Violet listened to her friend in awe. Considering how resistant Beatrice had been to spiritual concepts when they first met, since having her beautiful baby girl, Miracle, she had completely opened up and was really in tune with the spirit world around her. It was amazing.

"Finally, we need to look at our motivation. Why do we want a particular thing? What draws us to it? What helps us to move toward it? If we need something or someone to push us, then it's not necessarily the right thing for us."

The women were quiet for a moment, then Julie spoke up. "So you're saying that if we are focussed on what we want, but we're coming from a place of acceptance of what is, and we are drawn strongly toward it with no need to push ourselves, then it would just happen easily?"

Beatrice nodded. "Yes, I think so. The issue is that we are usually coming from a place of lack and resistance, or we are forcing ourselves to work toward something that we don't actually want, but we think we should want, or others say we should do."

Violet nodded. "I completely agree with that. I know when I have wanted something, but haven't felt at odds with my current reality, I have easily moved toward it and received it into my life with no problems."

"But how do we get into the state of acceptance of what is when we really don't like our situation? If we say – I love being broke, I love being single and lonely – aren't we just lying to ourselves and also focusing on what we don't want?" Lisa mused.

The women all laughed.

"I think the most important thing is to be completely honest and truthful to yourself," Violet said. "The word 'broke' has many connotations and negative energies around it, but in fact, you still have a roof over your head, enough money to pay the bills, clothes on your back and awesome friends around you. So you are by no means 'broke'. But you might feel that your income isn't as much as you would like – to give you the freedom to buy new clothes, eat healthier food or to go on holiday when you need it. Those things are true, but less heavy, less negative."

Lisa nodded. "So instead of saying – I love being single and lonely, I could say that I love having time to nurture myself, read good books and hang out with my awesome friends, and I would like to move toward finding someone I can share my life with."

"That sounds much better to me," Beatrice said. "Lighter and happier. You are happy where you are, and you are setting your intentions for the next step of your path."

There was a pause in the conversation, and Violet noticed empty cups and glasses. "Anyone for another cuppa or more wine?"

Everyone nodded and Amy got up to help her.

They went down to the kitchen and Violet put the kettle on. "So are you and Greg okay?" Amy asked.

Violet sighed. Her closest friend could always see right to the truth. "Yes, we're fine. Money has just been a little bit of an issue lately, which is why I called this meeting today. In truth, I was trying to get some ideas on how to get everything to flow a little better, and to work out why Earth Angels have so much trouble with finances."

Amy thought about it for a moment while she lined up the cups and took the cork out of a new bottle of wine.

"Sometimes I think that the financial struggles are a way to make us more focussed, more productive. I mean, we assume that if we didn't have to worry about money, we would have more time and energy to focus on the things that are most important to us, to be able to focus on our missions." Violet nodded in agreement and Amy continued. "But what if having plenty of money made us a little bit lazy instead? Made us more relaxed and less likely to pursue our missions? What if we were too busy shopping for clothes and shoes to be able to write our books and create classes and workshops to help others? After all, our desire to be of service to others comes from the desire to help and heal ourselves, which means that we need to be a little bit broken in order to do that."

Violet poured the hot water onto the teabags and sighed. "I have thought about that perspective, I have wondered if I would work so hard, push myself as much or have as much motivation if I didn't have to worry about money, and honestly, the answer is no, I wouldn't. There are days when I would quite happily just be here with Greg, eating tasty food, going for long walks, reading books and watching movies."

"That's because you're an Old Soul. You don't feel the need to achieve anything in this lifetime for yourself, because you've done it all before, many times over. And that's why I feel you have struggled with basic survival – to motivate you to create, to help others, to keep working hard."

Violet sighed. "I just feel so damned tired sometimes, Amy. I just want an easier ride for a while. I want enough money flowing in for me to be able to write the next book that is haunting me every night. Enough money so that Greg and I can hire some help when we need it. And enough money to have a weekend away. We haven't been away since our honeymoon and we both need the rest."

Amy smiled. "Speaking of honeymoons, there's something I've been meaning to tell you." She held out her left hand and Violet grabbed it and gasped.

"How didn't I notice this earlier? Oh my goodness, Angel! Congratulations! I'm so happy for you both."

Amy beamed with happiness and admired her ring that sparkled even in the dim kitchen light. "He asked me a few days ago, but I wanted to tell you in person. We're going to get married next year, but we haven't worked out all the details yet."

"That's wonderful news, I really couldn't be happier for you!"

Violet pulled Amy into a hug, but despite her genuine happiness for her best friend, couldn't help but feel a wave of sadness ripple through her. She tried to follow the feeling to see where it led, but couldn't work it out.

She shook it off and she and Amy took the hot drinks and wine upstairs to where the noise levels had risen. There seemed to be a raucous debate going on amongst the women as they argued over which type of Earth Angel made the best lover.

Violet joined in with the light-hearted banter, but the feeling of sadness stayed with her for the rest of the evening.

Chapter Two

"Starlight?"

"Emerald! How are you, beautiful Angel?"

The two Angels stood in the mists, in the veils between the two dimensions, where they overlapped, and dreamers often met their loved ones who had passed over.

"I'm well, enjoying being in the Angelic Realm with my Flame," Emerald replied.

Starlight smiled. "That's wonderful to hear. What have you called me here for? Only it's nearly morning and I know that Star will wake me shortly!"

Emerald nodded. "I won't keep you long. Mica has been wondering if we perhaps altered Velvet and Laguz's fates with our actions, and we wondered if it had any effect on the bigger picture. Have you looked at it recently? Is there any way that Mica and I could see it?"

Starlight frowned. "Are you sure you wish to see it? Seeing the bigger picture can really mess with your head."

"We know what happened on the original timeline, so it's not as though the ending will be a huge shock. We just wanted to see if anything had changed." Emerald waited patiently while the Angel of Destiny considered her request.

Finally, Starlight nodded. "Okay. But be sure that you don't start meddling with the timeline, whether your actions have changed things or not."

Emerald nodded in agreement.

Starlight looked down at her hand, and then closed her eyes and concentrated. When she opened her eyes, a small bottle filled with an indigo blue liquid containing silver lights sat in the palm of her hand. She smiled and handed it to Emerald.

"Pour this into the lake, and you will be shown the bigger picture as it is now."

Emerald looked down at the bottle, feeling awe that such a small vessel could hold such a vast amount of information. "Thank you. I understand that this is a huge thing to entrust us with, and I appreciate it. I will let you get back to your family."

Emerald took a step back, but Starlight stopped her from leaving.

"Wait, can you give something to Gold for me, too?"

Starlight looked down at her hand again, and this time an even smaller vial, containing shimmering pink liquid appeared. She gave it to Emerald.

"I will make sure he receives this," Emerald assured her, clutching the vial tightly.

"Thank you, Angel. Don't hesitate to call upon me again if you need me."

They hugged, and then Emerald left the mists between the dimensions and returned to where Mica stood at the gates to the Angelic Realm.

"Did you see her?" he asked when she landed gently next to him.

"Yes. She gave me this." She handed the bottle of indigo liquid to him. "When poured into the lake, it will show us the bigger picture."

Mica's eyes widened. "That's amazing. Let's do it."

Emerald shook her head. "I must deliver something to Gold first. Why don't you go ahead to the lake, and I will join you in a few moments."

Mica smiled and kissed her quickly. "I'll see you soon."

Emerald nodded and headed off to where the Elder would be stationed, welcoming souls from Earth to the Other Side.

*   *   *

"Emerald! To what do I owe this pleasure?"

When the Angel smiled, he detected a sadness in her expression. His heart stuttered. Was something wrong with Starlight?

"I have just met with Starlight, in the dream mists," the Angel began, causing Gold's heart to stall momentarily, as she confirmed his fears.

"Is she okay?" he asked, afraid to hear the answer.

"She's very well. I had a favour to ask her, and in return she asked me to do one for her."

Gold frowned, and his heart returned to normal. "What was the favour she wished?"

Emerald held out the tiny vial of shimmering pink liquid to him, and he took it from her, curiously examining it. When the glass vial itself gave away no clues, he frowned at the Angel. "What is it?"

Emerald looked puzzled. "Oh, I assumed you would know what to do with it. I think if you pour it into the lake, something will happen. Starlight didn't give me any instructions."

"The lake? Can it be any water?"

Emerald shrugged. "I guess."

Gold waved his hand and the mist in front of him began to swirl. He took the stopper out of the vial and poured a drop of the liquid into the swirl. In the blink of an eye, the swirling mist turned pink, and then formed the shape of a woman with long blonde hair.

"Starlight!" Gold gasped, nearly dropping the vial with the remaining liquid in it. Emerald quickly took it from him and put the stopper back in.

"Gold," the apparition of Starlight said. "My love, I hope this message finds you well."

Gold frowned. It appeared this was simply a recorded message and was not interactive.

"I sense there are great shifts occurring in the world, and the time of the harmonious reunion of all Flames is near. As such, I believe, my dear Gold, it is time for you to consider fulfilling the ancient prophecies."

Gold's eyes widened, and he saw Emerald frowning at him. He shook his head. "But Starlight, I can't, you know I must-"

"I know you will be protesting right now," Starlight said, chuckling, "But I am deaf to your resistance. I know it is possible because I have seen it. I know it is necessary, because I can feel it. Please begin doing what is needed to make it a reality. The world needs you, my love. I will see you soon."

The mists swirled around Starlight's form, and she dissipated.

"What is she talking about? What are the ancient prophecies?"

Gold took the vial of pink liquid back, wondering if there were more messages, or if each drop contained the same message.

"A true Heaven on Earth."

"How does she want you to create that?"

Gold looked the Angel in the eye. "By going to Earth and creating it myself."

*　*　*

"How was Gold?" Mica enquired when Emerald joined him on the shore of the lake.

Emerald smiled. "He was good. A little shocked though."

"About what?"

"I delivered a vial to him, from Starlight, which contained a message that basically said he needed to go to Earth."

Mica raised his eyebrows. "Gold, going to Earth? Do you realise how momentous that is? How much that will change things?"

Emerald nodded. "It is a massive shift from the old timeline. So even if we look at the timeline as it currently is, if Gold goes to Earth, it will no doubt change again."

Mica looked down at the bottle in his hand. "Shall we wait then, to look?"

Emerald shook her head and smiled. She took the bottle from him and removed the stopper. She held the bottle over the lake and tapped out a single drop which contained a single silver light within it, into the still water below. The drop hit the water and created a ripple that moved outward, darkening the surface of the water.

"We can use a single drop at a time. This way, we can see if the many shifts happening do actually change the timeline."

She replaced the stopper and tucked it safely into her robes, then they both looked into the inky darkness of the lake.

"What will we see?" Mica whispered.

"I have no idea," Emerald replied.

Chapter Three

"So did you come up with the miracle cure to scarcity last night?" Greg asked Violet as she entered the kitchen the next morning.

Violet kissed him on the head as she passed by on her way to the kettle. "Not entirely, though some good stuff was discussed. I'm sorry you were asleep by the time I got to bed, you know what we're like once we get started."

Greg got up from the kitchen stool and came over to her, wrapping his arms around her waist, then resting his head on her shoulder. "I'm sorry I couldn't stay up. You know I love to fall asleep holding you."

Violet smiled and breathed in his scent, knowing that if she could just bottle moments like this, she would be able to get through all the tough parts of her life with ease and grace.

"I love falling asleep in your arms," Violet replied. "I like doing other stuff too."

Greg chuckled, and his breath against her ear made her shiver with delight. "It's still pretty early..."

Violet turned around and kissed him deeply. "Let's go back to bed," she whispered.

Greg grinned and took her hand and led her back up to the bedroom. Once the door was closed behind them, Violet slid her pyjama bottoms and tank top off, and Greg pulled off his t-shirt and underwear. They stood for a few moments, appreciating each other, until Violet couldn't resist the magnetism any longer and reached out to Greg to pull him onto the bed.

When Violet looked into Greg's eyes after they fell into an exhausted heap under the covers, she couldn't help thinking that it was a good thing they didn't have any neighbours close by and there wasn't a retreat in session.

Violet closed her eyes, and suddenly found herself in a flashback to another time, another life, when she and her Flame were wrapped up in each other's arms. A feeling of peace tinged with sadness washed over her, and she felt a tear fall from the corner of her eye.

"Hey, what is it?" Greg asked, smoothing the errant tear with his thumb.

Violet shook her head. "Nothing, I just had a flashback to being in bed with you, though your eyes were green then. It made me feel a bit sad, but I don't know why."

"You're sad that I don't have green eyes?"

Violet laughed. Greg always knew how to diffuse any negativity and make her smile.

"No, silly. I don't know why it made me sad."

Greg smiled. "Perhaps I was a better lover then, and you were mourning my past incarnation."

Violet started giggling and found that she couldn't stop. Greg soon joined in, unable to resist the infectious laughter. By the time they could calm themselves down they both had tears streaming down their cheeks, and there was someone hammering on the front door.

Greg kissed Violet and leapt out of bed to throw on some clothes to answer the door. Violet closed her eyes, tempted to fall asleep again, but when she heard the voices downstairs and recognised them as Lisa's and Amy's, she sighed and pulled the covers back, then went to the bathroom to freshen up before pulling on some clothes and going down to greet her friends.

Amy raised an eyebrow at her bed hair and dishevelled clothing. She turned to Lisa. "I told you we were probably disturbing them."

Lisa blushed bright red. "Sorry, Violet, sorry, Greg, I was

just so excited to share all the insights that came through last night, I just assumed you guys would be up by now."

"We were up," Greg said. "We just, um, yeah. Anyway, it's cool, I need to get on with some stuff." He kissed Violet on the cheek then left the house, presumably to hide in his man cave (also known as his workshop) while the women talked.

Violet refilled the kettle before boiling it. She pulled three mugs out and got out her friends' favourite teas, then poured them before taking a seat at the breakfast bar with them. She was really hungry now, on account of it being past ten o'clock, but she wanted to hear what Lisa had to say before making breakfast.

"So, after last night's meeting, my mind was whirling with all of the possibilities and reasons why Earth Angels find it so difficult to manifest money and to keep our finances in order, and when I finally got to sleep, my dreams were incredibly vivid, and I'm pretty sure that I travelled back to Atlantis."

Violet smiled. "I had a mini flashback to Atlantis this morning too. There must be some interesting energies in the air."

"This dream was quite brief, but it was very particular and detailed." Lisa took a sip of her tea, and Violet leaned forward. When the pause lasted a few moments too long, she looked at Amy, who was smiling.

"Well? What happened?" she asked. "Don't keep me in suspense, you know I hate it."

Lisa and Amy grinned at each other. They did know that.

"I'm stalling because now, repeating it again, to you, it just feels a bit silly."

Violet frowned. "If Amy already knows, then you have to tell me!"

"Okay, okay. I could see how matter was created in Atlantis."

Violet felt her eyebrows raise, and couldn't bring them back down before Lisa noticed.

"See? I told you it sounded mad."

"No, don't mind me, continue, what do you mean that you could see how matter was created?"

"I mean that I remember seeing how things were brought into

existence from the nothingness. I could see all the layers of the different dimensions, and how we used to bring forth material, physical matter from the dimension of pure potentiality."

Violet blinked. "I think I need to eat something." She hopped off the stool and started pulling out pancake ingredients from the cupboard. She waved for Lisa to continue while she cooked. She could feel a weird fluttering in her stomach, but couldn't tell if it was from hunger or excitement.

"So we were stood in a circle – myself, you, Greg, and four other elders of Atlantis, and we all held the same point of focus, the same thought, and projected that thought onto a table in the centre of the circle. I could see the energy of our thoughts, our focus, and it created a miniature whirlwind of energy above the table, and after a few moments, it stopped, and there, on the table, as though it had been there the whole time, was a tablet."

Violet paused in the act of breaking an egg into the flour and frowned at Lisa. "A tablet? Of stone? Or do you mean a pill?"

Lisa smiled. "No, I mean like an iPad."

Violet burst out laughing. "In Atlantis? Are you sure your dream wasn't just about manifesting what you want now?"

Lisa shook her head. "No, it definitely happened in Atlantis. We created the technology that we have in our world currently. Remember, Atlanteans originated from other planets, with technology far more advanced than on Earth. All we did, as a group, was to concentrate that energy into a focussed point which created physical matter."

Violet stirred some water into the flour to make the pancake batter and tried to take on board Lisa's words, but it just seemed too fantastical. Even for someone who believed in Faeries.

"And you think that we can do that too? In this life? Bring physical matter into being through focussed thought?"

"Yes, I do."

"I do, too," Amy chimed in, finishing her mug of tea. "After all, isn't that what the whole law of attraction craze was about? Creating things with our thoughts?"

"Yes, but not out of the air, out of nothing." Violet put the frying pan on the gas ring, added some coconut oil, then when it was hot enough, added some batter. The familiar task of making pancakes was helping to keep her hands busy while her mind raced with the possibilities of what Lisa was suggesting.

"If we had iPads in Atlantis, then how come we didn't contact the outside world for help? Why couldn't we save Atlantis?"

Lisa shrugged. "I guess the internet didn't exist yet," she said, a smile on her face.

Violet laughed. "Yeah. I guess a tablet would have been fairly useless without electricity or the internet, so why did we create it? Why did we call it forth? Why not create food, or medicine, or something useful?"

Lisa thought about it for a moment. "I think the idea was to create something that didn't yet exist. To prove that it had not merely been transported from somewhere else, that we had actually created it with our minds."

Violet flipped the first pancake in the pan and nodded. "Yes, I can see that we would have decided on that. I think back then things appearing from one place to another may have seemed quite simple."

She picked out some fruit from the fridge and washed it to accompany the pancakes. "So when are we going to give it a try? Do we need seven people?"

Lisa glanced at Amy then back to Violet. "Try? You mean you want to sit around a table and create something out of thin air?"

Violet laughed. "Isn't that why you just told us about your dream? And if at least three of us are originals from Atlantis, then we should be able to recreate the energy, don't you think?"

"I'm up for it!" Amy said, coming over to Violet to receive the first pancake.

"Could you take that out to Greg?" Violet asked her friend. Amy nodded and grabbed a fork before heading out to Greg's workshop with his breakfast.

Lisa took her mug over to the kettle to make another drink, while Violet started the next pancake. "What if nothing happens though? What if it was just a silly dream, the product of my overactive imagination?"

"Did it feel that way?" Violet asked.

Lisa shook her head. "No, it felt very real."

"Then where's the harm in trying? If nothing happens, nothing happens, no big deal." Violet flipped the pancake and Lisa poured the hot water onto her teabag.

"Okay, when shall we do it?"

"Tonight? We're still under the influence of the new moon which I think will help to amplify our energy. I will call Lisa, Beatrice and Julie, to see if they're free again. Depends on the guys watching the kids, of course."

Lisa sat down at the breakfast bar and Violet set the pancake on a plate in front of her and gestured for her to take some fruit.

"Do you think it could work?" Lisa asked her.

Violet shrugged and the words of an old friend came to mind. "Anything is possible."

* * *

Long after the lake had returned to normal, Emerald and Mica sat staring at the water in silence. It seemed that neither of them knew how to respond to seeing the bigger picture of the fate of the human civilisation.

Finally, Mica broke the silence.

"What can we do?"

Emerald's mind was a blur. "I'm not sure. I mean, I thought that perhaps the new timeline would differ a little to the old one, but not quite this much. We truly did underestimate the power that Velvet's return would have on the world. Just as we underestimated her while she taught at the Academy."

"I'm sure she will forgive us," Mica said with a wry smile.

Emerald smiled back. "Do you think there are other Angels here who know just how much things have shifted? Because it seems to me that if they knew, then things would shift even more so, because their energy would be entirely different when helping those on Earth."

Mica frowned. "Are we allowed to make this knowledge known? Was Starlight okay with that? Usually, messing with fate and destiny is reserved for the Elders, and even they steer clear of it when they can."

Emerald thought of Starlight's caution, and in that moment, rebelled against her inbuilt moral compass. "She didn't say we couldn't tell anyone." She winced internally at her lie, and hoped the Angel of Destiny would understand.

"Wow, okay, then I guess we can ask around, find out if anyone else knows of the shifts."

This time it was Emerald who stood up and offered her hand to her Flame.

"Where shall we go first?"

Emerald thought for a moment. "I have an idea."

Chapter Four

"So, what do you think?"

Violet looked around the circle of her five friends and Greg, all of whom were sat cross-legged on cushions in the upstairs workshop room.

The group each glanced at one another, looks of excitement and scepticism on their faces.

"I know it sounds really mad," Lisa said. "But the dream was incredibly vivid, and so we figured it was worth a shot."

"What are we going to manifest?" Beatrice asked, her eyes wide in curiosity. "I mean, can any of us imagine something that doesn't yet exist?"

They all looked at each other, and Greg spoke up.

"How about a machine that can record our thoughts, or dreams? That doesn't exist yet, does it?"

"I want one of those!" Lisa said. "That sounds awesome."

"I can imagine that," Beatrice agreed.

"Great," Velvet said with a grin. "Let's do it. We will all focus on this small tray," she tapped the brown tray in the centre of their circle. "And we will imagine a machine that can record our dreams. Not thoughts. Recording thoughts sounds too scary."

Everyone chuckled and agreed. Violet instructed them to take three deep breaths, then they all stared at the empty tray, each imagining a machine being created from the field of pure potentiality, and seeing it manifest right before them.

After five minutes, Velvet could feel her eyelids drooping and her legs beginning to go to sleep. She closed her eyes just for a moment, and was surprised to be gently awoken half an hour later.

She blinked at Greg who was smiling at her. "What happened?"

"Apparently we all fell asleep," he replied.

Velvet looked around her friends who were all yawning and blinking. She looked at the tray, which was still empty.

"Did anyone see anything?" She asked.

Everyone shook their heads.

"Was in a very deep, meditative sleep," Lisa said, stretching. "But no, I didn't see anything."

"Should we try again?" Violet asked.

"I'm starving, actually, I don't think I could concentrate with my stomach rumbling." Julie admitted.

"I need to get back home," Beatrice said. "We could try again soon though."

Violet felt a bit disappointed that nothing had happened, but nodded and got up slowly. "I have cakes and drinks downstairs, everyone should eat something before driving, I feel oddly hungry too."

They all went downstairs, and Violet put the kettle on. Greg went outside to do more work in his workshop, and after a quick cuppa and a piece of cake, everyone left, and Violet curled up on the sofa with her second cup of tea, thinking over the evening and wondering what they could do to make the process work. Perhaps it was something that had only worked in Atlantis. Maybe the energy on Earth was just too dense now. She was staring at the wall, lost deep in her thoughts when Greg came back inside.

"Hey, are you okay?"

She smiled up at him. "Yes, just thinking about whether we could improve the process to make it work. Feeling both disappointed it didn't work and a bit silly for thinking it would."

"It was only our first try," Greg said, settling on the sofa beside her and wrapping an arm around her shoulders. "I don't think we can call the idea a complete failure yet."

"Yeah, I know. I'm just impatient I guess."

"I know. It does feel like things take far too long to manifest on this planet. I'm ready for things to start flowing too. But I was thinking about what Beatrice said about resisting reality, and being at war with our own reality. I realised that I have been at war with my own for a very long time. I never feel like I have done enough, that I am where I want to be, or that things are flowing. I always want to be somewhere I'm not."

Violet frowned. "You don't want to be here?"

"Of course I want to be here, I want to be with you, but I hate that we still struggle with finances, I hate that we haven't been able to progress our relationship, and it feels like there is a never-ending list of things that need sorting, fixing and making. It feels like I'm on a hamster wheel, desperately trying to get to somewhere I'm never going to reach."

Violet frowned, her heart feeling heavy as she listened to Greg's words. She hadn't realised he struggled with the way things were.

"What can we do to change things so they're more acceptable?" she asked, trying not to take it personally that he was unhappy.

"I think I need to accept the way things are, and focus on how I would like them to be. Rather that fighting what is. But I'm not entirely sure how to do that, or what it would look like to do that."

The words of Violet's old neighbour came back to her and she smiled and reached up to kiss Greg. "The *how* is not up to us, it's up to God. Let go of the *how* and focus on the *what.*"

"How come I'm married to such a wise soul? It's kind of annoying sometimes, you know."

Violet giggled. "I know, sorry, I guess you'll just have to accept it. There's no point in resisting, after all."

Greg growled and tickled her side, making Violet shriek and jump up off the sofa. Greg leapt up after her and wrapped her in his arms. "I love you exactly the way you are," he said, suddenly becoming serious.

Violet looked up into his eyes and smiled. "I love you exactly the way you are too."

"Even though I don't have green eyes?"

Violet giggled and reached up to kiss him, and all sadness and heaviness melted away.

*　*　*

"Who told you where to find me?"

The tall Angel with huge brown wings towered over Emerald and Mica, but neither of them felt threatened by his presence, his energy was much too benevolent.

"Galena from the Angelic Assistance Team said she'd heard rumours that there were Angels working on a new mission, and that you were leading them," Mica said. "We have discovered new information which we thought might be of some use to you, and we would like to help."

The Angel frowned. "It seems that secrets are impossible to keep in this realm."

Emerald chuckled. "Indeed. Sometimes I think we Angels are worse than the Faeries when it comes to talking. But believe me when I say that our interest in your work is for the higher good. We have a strong connection to many souls on Earth right now, and we would so much like to ensure they are able to fulfil their missions and that they help to change the fate of the world."

The Angel still didn't look convinced, his arms crossed tightly over his chest. Emerald could see that a different approach would be needed.

"Aragonite," she said softly, reaching out to touch his arm. "We have been watching Earth, and one of the souls we wish to help is your Flame, Blue."

His arms loosened and his expression softened. "You know my Blue?"

"She has found Velvet and Laguz. She is assisting them in reuniting the Flames, and she is fulfilling her mission. But we fear that without our assistance she, and many other Earth

Angels, will become overwhelmed by their tasks and they will give up and go back to sleep."

Aragonite smiled, and his whole body relaxed. "Any friend of Blue's is a friend of mine. Please, come with me." He ushered them through the door behind him, which led them through a dark corridor, quite unlike the light of the Angelic Realm.

They followed him for a few minutes, before they reached another door. When they stepped through, both Emerald and Mica gasped at the sight of a cavern full of more than a hundred Angels, arranged in several small circles, all intensely staring into their own small vessels of water.

"What are they doing?" Emerald whispered.

"They are altering the current reality, one tiny drop at a time," Aragonite replied.

Mica frowned. "Does Pallas know about this? Or the Elders?"

Aragonite raised an eyebrow. "Since when do the Angels of the higher realms need permission to do their work?" When neither Angel replied, Aragonite sighed. "Fear not, this entire mission was created by one of the most powerful Elders in the Universe. We are not breaking the laws of the Universe, nor taking away the free will of the humans."

Emerald wondered if the Angel he spoke of was Starlight. Surely she was the only one powerful enough to create this.

"But Pallas and the Elders don't know about it?" Mica asked again.

Aragonite shook his head. "No, which is why I need to pay Galena a visit and request that she respectfully keep the rumours to herself. What we are doing here is a very fragile operation, and I would hate for us to be forced to stop now."

"So what exactly are they doing? How did this all start?" Mica couldn't hide his curiosity.

Aragonite motioned for them to follow him away from the enormous room filled with murmuring Angels to a smaller room filled with cushions. Aragonite was so tall he had to duck under the doorframe, and they followed him inside and closed the door behind them.

"Make yourselves comfortable," he said, sitting down on

a mountain of soft pillows. They did the same, and waited for him to begin.

"Not long ago, I was one of many Angels who volunteered to go to distant planets in other Universes and Galaxies that were spinning out of control. We were asked by the Elders to restore peace and order to these planets, to prevent them from being destroyed. Much like the Earth Angels are doing on Earth right now." Aragonite sighed. "It seemed like a good mission, I even gave up the opportunity to be with Blue in order to help, but when we arrived on the planets, it was quite clear, very quickly, that we would be ineffective in changing things. So the Elders called upon Starlight to assist. The programmes she created, were similar to that which you see here. A team of Angels making minute changes on a constant basis that will alter the course of their destiny. It worked on the first planet, and then the second, and as I was responsible for the teams of Angels involved, I got to speak with Starlight, and I asked her if it would be possible to do the same thing with Earth."

Mica raised his hand hesitantly, not wanting to interrupt, but he had a burning question to ask.

"Yes?" Aragonite asked.

"Isn't Starlight on Earth? How was she also in other Universes?"

"Though Gold and the other Elders tried to get her to return to the Other Side to complete this work, she found a way to do so astrally. While her body slept on Earth, her soul was travelling through the Universes, carrying out this work."

"Oh," Mica said. "I understand. Please, continue."

Aragonite nodded. "Starlight was intrigued by the idea. In the past Angels have always played a background role assisting humans in ways that did not interfere with their free will. But not long ago, there was a mission, founded by Pallas and Gold, for a team of Angels to go to Earth in human form, to change events and save lives. After their many missions on Earth, a shift in the timeline was perceived, and so Starlight felt that if we were to do on Earth what we have been doing on other planets, it would change the destiny of the world."

Emerald frowned. She wondered if the reason that Starlight

had told her not to meddle with the timeline and therefore the bigger picture, wasn't because it was a bad idea, or messed with destiny, but because she already had a huge team of Angels doing just that. "So you are essentially playing a cosmic game of chess with humans as the pawns?"

Aragonite raised an eyebrow. "I wouldn't say that we were playing with anyone, we are just giving souls a slightly stronger nudge than the Angels on the Angelic Assistance Team are currently able to give. We are directing them onto the path of their true destiny, and in doing so, we are altering the destiny of the world as a whole."

Emerald considered his words, and then considered his genuine authority. She had no doubt that he truly believed that the work they were undertaking was for the benefit of all humankind.

Aragonite looked at them both. "So what was the information you have, that might help?"

Emerald's hand went automatically to the bottle in her robes. Despite her internal reservations, she did trust the Angel before her. "I also spoke with Starlight recently, and she gave me something that enabled us to see the bigger picture. I wondered why she gave it to me so easily, but I think perhaps she knew that we would join forces and do what needed to be done to change the timeline." She pulled out the bottle and handed it to Aragonite. "A single drop in water will show you the entire destiny of Earth. Mica and I have seen it, and we know, having lived through the first timeline, that it has shifted quite a lot, and we believe that it is entirely possible to shift it so that the Golden Age is actually possible, and even perhaps that the world won't end in the way it did before."

Aragonite stared down at the bottle of indigo liquid, the silver lights sparkling in the dimly lit room. "This is what we have been in need of. A way to gauge whether our actions here are being effective." He looked at them both, a smile lighting up his whole face. "Thank you, this will be very useful indeed. Was there anything else?"

The two Angels shook their heads. They had already decided they would keep Starlight's message to Gold about the ancient prophecies a secret for now. Neither of them wanted to raise any hopes, only to dash them again if Gold decided not to go to Earth.

"We want to be a part of it, we want to help. We don't wish to just sit around, watching what happens," Mica said.

Aragonite nodded. "As it happens, there are a couple of spaces available on the team. I would be honoured if you joined us."

"Could we focus our efforts on the reunion of the Flames?" Emerald asked. "It was our mission on Earth, and it is something we are both very passionate about."

Aragonite nodded. "That sounds like a great idea. I will introduce you to the Twin Flame Team, they will be able to fill you in on their action plan."

Emerald smiled. "Thank you. Thank you for trusting us, and for welcoming us here to help you, I promise we will do everything we can."

Aragonite nodded. "I know you will."

Chapter Five

"What do you think it takes to create a harmonious Twin Flame relationship?"

Violet considered the question of one of her retreat participants for a moment before answering. "That's a great question," she mused.

"Do you do classes on that? You have retreats for finding your Flame, retreats for those who have lost their Flames, and for those who wish to move on, but what about those who are with their Flames and who want to make sure it works and is a happy relationship?"

Violet smiled. "I believe you may have just inspired a brand new retreat right there. Why don't we discuss what everyone feels makes a happy Twin Flame relationship? I mean, I have some idea from my own experience, but I would love to hear what you all think."

A shy lady called Kristal raised her hand, and Violet motioned for her to go first.

"I feel that being on an equal footing is really important. My Flame and I were completely unequal when it came to finances and emotional support from friends and family, and the imbalance definitely played a part in our break up."

Violet nodded, and realising that it might be a good idea to take notes, she got up and quickly grabbed a pen and a notepad from the side table and jotted down what Kristal had just said.

"I hadn't thought of the emotional support thing," Jane, another participant said thoughtfully. "My Flame had so many friends to go out with, to talk to, and I had no one. I was so focussed on him that I fell out of touch with all my family and friends, and then when things were rough, I had no one to talk to. Which meant that I vented everything onto him, which made the whole situation worse. I think that's why he'd had enough in the end. If I'd had a circle of friends like this to talk to, we might have been able to heal our problems."

Violet made a few extra notes and nodded. "Being in a Twin Flame relationship can be really intense, and it can be too easy to become so wrapped up in each other that it's difficult to make time for others. But it is important to take the time to continue nurturing relationships and friendships outside of the Twin Flame union, and to give each other the space to explore and evolve too."

The discussion continued for another hour, by the end of which, Violet had several pages of notes with which to create a new retreat. She felt both excited and exhausted by the idea. She set her notebook down and announced it was lunchtime, as her nostrils had picked up the scent of soup wafting up the stairs to where they were sat in the workshop room.

The women all headed downstairs, chattering noisily as they settled into the dining area, while Violet headed to the kitchen to see if Greg needed any help.

"Perfect timing," Greg said as he got seven bowls out of the cupboard and began ladling soup into them.

Violet took the first bowl of soup from him, wiped the edge with a tea towel, then turned and kissed him quickly before he filled the next.

"You okay?" he asked.

She smiled. He read her so easily. He knew that something was up with her, sometimes before she even knew it herself.

"Yeah, I'm okay, was just an interesting session. A new retreat idea came up." Violet took the second bowl of soup and headed out to the dining room, and served the first two ladies. The fresh, homemade bread was already on the table, and the women began eating immediately.

Violet returned to the kitchen where two more bowls of soup awaited. She went back and forth until all of her retreat participants had their food, then she returned to the kitchen to sit and eat with Greg.

"What was the idea? I'm intrigued," Greg said, dunking his bread in the soup before biting into it.

"A retreat on how to have a happy Twin Flame relationship. On what it takes to sustain the union and thrive within it."

Greg nodded as he chewed and swallowed his bread. "Sounds like a good idea. There must be some Twin Flames who are in happy relationships, perhaps you could interview them?"

Violet raised an eyebrow. "You don't think we know enough on the subject?"

"Well, sure," Greg said, shrugging. "But we can't base the retreats purely off our own experience, we need to do a little more research than that, surely?"

Violet ate a spoonful of soup. He had a point, but somehow it didn't feel like he was telling the whole story. "Are you happy?" she asked.

Greg put his spoon down, and turned to Violet. Keeping his voice low so they wouldn't be overheard by the women in the other room, he replied, "Mostly, but I still have doubts, and fears."

"About what?" Violet asked, setting her own spoon down and giving him her full attention.

"About us, about what we're doing here. I don't know if I'm living my purpose, my mission. And I don't know if you are, either."

Even though she had asked, and she genuinely had wanted to know, she felt like she had been slapped across the face. "I see," she said, unsure what to say.

"I love you, I love being with you, I love what we're doing here, but it doesn't feel like enough. It just feels like I'm spending my days chopping wood, fixing things and cooking and cleaning. And it feels like you spend most of your time stressing out over making enough money and changing beds and hosting. You should be writing. I can see that clearly. You have more books to write."

"And you, what do you want to be doing?"

Greg shrugged. "I don't know yet, I feel like I need to explore some ideas, try some new things." He sighed. "I think about Esmeralda and Mike a lot. And I don't want us to head down the same path. Esmeralda got sick because she was burnt out, and Mike, well, I think Mike just couldn't be here without her, which I can completely understand."

"I'm not going to get cancer and die, if that's what you're worried about. I mean, we eat healthily, we exercise, and-"

"We never take time off, rarely relax and aren't doing what we love," Greg finished.

Violet sighed. She turned her head to the other room and realised it had gone very quiet in there; she hoped the women couldn't hear their conversation.

"What do you suggest we do then?" she whispered, trying to eat some more soup, even though she felt like she had a hard lump in the pit of her stomach.

"I don't know yet. Perhaps we just need some space to figure out what we really want."

Violet's eyes widened and her heart thudded. "Are you saying what I think you're saying?"

Greg closed his eyes. "Let's talk about this after the retreat. I'm sorry, I didn't want to upset you while you're working."

Violet stood up abruptly from the breakfast bar and took her half-empty soup bowl and remaining bread to the sink. She placed them down, took a deep breath, plastered a smile on her face then turned on her heel and went out to see if the women had finished their meal, and if they were ready to watch a movie. She avoided looking at Greg as she passed him, and used all of her strength and willpower not to burst into tears.

She silently called on the Angels to give her the courage and strength to finish running the retreat, and to help her work out what exactly she was meant to do now.

"So," she said brightly to the women in the front dining room. "Who's up for a film?"

* * *

Emerald watched the exchange between her two friends, before turning to the Angel next to her. "Benit, I fear that my friends, two very powerful Old Souls, instrumental to the Awakening, may be about to part ways. Last time it happened, it was catastrophic to the fate of the planet. What would you suggest I do to change their course?"

Benit leaned over to look into Emerald's pool of water, and watched the two of them for a while. "It is a tricky thing with Flames, as I am sure you are well aware. Sometimes, space is absolutely necessary for their evolution and growth, and to enable them to work through past baggage that may impede their future together."

Emerald nodded, but still feared a repeat of the original timeline.

"I have watched over Velvet and Laguz before, and in fact, the Atlantis Angel Team have been working with their circle of friends recently, to remind them of the manifesting techniques they once knew. I believe that both souls are in quite a different place to the previous split, and would actually be okay if they were to spend some time apart. I think I would get a trusted friend of Velvet's to encourage her to follow her own path for a while. To see if the space inspires changes that will be beneficial to the timeline."

"You want me to encourage them to split up?" Emerald was aghast. Her mission had always been to reunite the Flames, not break them up.

"It doesn't have to be for long. But a short while away from each other may actually strengthen their bond, making it unbreakable in all dimensions and worlds."

Emerald sighed. She could see the Angel's reasoning, but the idea of hurting her friend in that way, hurt her.

"This work is not easy. And in truth, we do not know if our actions are helping or hurting the destiny of the world. We can only make the best decisions we can, based on our wisdom and our knowledge of the bigger picture. As we saw from Aragonite showing us all the current bigger picture, we have already seen changes. Positive changes." He patted Emerald on the arm. "Just have faith in yourself, and in your intuition of the situation. You cannot go wrong."

Emerald nodded and tried to smile, but her heart still hurt. "Thank you." She looked back down at the still water, and closed her eyes to send her intention to Velvet's best friend, hoping that if the Old Soul ever found out what she was about to do, she would one day be able to forgive her.

*　　*　　*

"He said what?"

Violet sighed. "I know, it's like déjà vu all over again," she said to her best friend as they walked down the hill to the river. "I kept getting flashbacks to that day at the campsite in France when he told me he no longer wanted to be with me."

Amy shook her head. "That day was awful, I would quite happily live the rest of my life not having to go through that again."

"Ditto," Violet replied. "I just don't see how us being apart from each other will help us to find our missions, to live our purpose. I mean, surely helping the Twin Flames is a beautiful purpose? It will be the unconditional love of the Flames that brings this world into the Golden Age."

"Yeah I guess so," Amy said, bending down to pick up an unusual shaped twig from the ground.

Violet frowned. "You don't seem so convinced?"

Amy studied the twig which looked a little like a magic wand and shrugged. "I think it's amazing what you're doing, and I know that all of the Flames you help are really appreciative, but…"

"But?"

"It doesn't seem like enough."

Violet stopped in her tracks and turned to her friend. "Have you spoken to Greg about this?"

Amy looked up at her and shook her head. "No, why?"

"Because that's exactly what Greg said. That what we are doing is not enough."

"Maybe it really isn't then. Do you feel fulfilled right now? Do you feel like you're living your purpose?"

Violet breathed in deeply then continued walking down the path. She thought about her friend's question. Did she feel fulfilled? Was she living her purpose?

She wanted to answer immediately, and say – yes of course she was, on both counts – but there was a feeling in the pit of her stomach that stopped her. She breathed into the questions and allowed herself to listen out for the answers from deep within. Even though a part of her screamed that it didn't want to know the truth.

They had reached the river at the bottom of the hill before she answered her best friend.

"No. I don't feel that I am," she said softly.

Her friend nodded, and sat down on a smooth rock at the water's edge. The river was flowing smoothly and calmly, and glittered in the late afternoon sunlight.

"What would fulfil you? What is your purpose?"

Violet stared out at the water, and again, breathed deeply into the questions. It took a while to get past the chatter of her conscious mind, to get past the logical answers, the expected answers, to find the real answers buried deep down within her.

"My purpose is to step into the truth of who I am, to manifest and create consciously with all I do and say, and to help others to do the same."

"What does that look like?" Amy asked.

Violet breathed deeply and closed her eyes to visualise what it would look like to be fully in her truth. "I would be talking to more people, I would be writing more books. I would be reminding the Earth Angels where they have come from, and who they really are."

"So similar to what you are doing now, but just on a bigger scale? To a larger audience?"

"I guess." Violet opened her eyes and the image of herself on a stage talking to thousands faded away into the water. "It scares me though, to think of doing bigger things, to go beyond the retreats and to reach more people."

Amy frowned. "Why is it scary?"

"Because it's putting myself in an exposed position. I like being hidden away here in the woods." Violet waved her hand at the trees surrounding them where they sat.

Amy smiled, she knew how Violet felt. They had been friends for many years in this life, and in many lifetimes before that.

"You need to find a way to channel Velvet more often. She taught thousands of Earth Angels, ran an entire Academy, and conversed with the Elders. Not to mention being the Angel of Fate."

Violet sighed. "She had fears too though. I could feel that when I wrote the book about the Academy. She doubted her ability to teach, she couldn't see the bigger picture. I feel as though I am just repeating her mistakes and still feeling her doubts."

"Well you are her, so that would make sense. But I think it may be time to clear those issues, and create something new. Now is not the time to hide. The world is getting darker, angrier, and more violent. It needs you to stand up and bring light into the darkness, not hide in the shadows, hoping not to be noticed."

Violet sighed. "Why do you keep making so much sense?"

"Because I am an Angel. We always make a lot of sense. And we have an easier time seeing the bigger picture. I understand you wanting to remain safe and cosy here in the woods with Greg. After all, it's not like you two have really had a decent amount of time together, your time was cut short in Atlantis, you had just days in the Academy, and now you've had eleven years. It's really not fair that you guys haven't had more time than that together, but it doesn't mean that you won't have more time together in the future. This could just be for a short time."

Violet blinked at her friend, tears filling her eyes before she could stop it. "It sounds like you're saying we should break up?"

Amy sighed. "I'm saying that you both may need some space in order to move forward. In order to follow your mission, and for Greg to discover his."

Violet allowed the tears to fall freely, and her heart ached at the idea of leaving her Flame. She stood up suddenly, knowing that she needed to be back at the house, in his arms. Amy followed her as she strode back to the path, away from the river.

The tears fell all the way back up the hill, leaving Violet short of breath when they arrived back at the house. Greg was outside, covered in sawdust. He smiled at Violet and Amy as they approached, but his smile turned into a frown when he saw Violet's face.

"What's wro-"

He was cut off by Violet kissing him hard on the lips, her hands either side of his face, her body pressed against his. Her tears wet his cheeks, and when he responded, kissing her back, the tears flowed even faster.

Because in that moment, she knew that her Angel friend was right.

*   *   *

Emerald felt the comforting arms of her Flame wrap around her waist, and the tears streamed faster down her cheeks.

"My dear love, what's wrong?" Mica whispered in her ear.

Emerald bowed her head. "I have just helped to initiate the separation of Velvet and Laguz, and my heart feels broken. When I think of the times we have been apart, I remember the pain I felt, and I cannot believe I am playing a part in creating that pain in my dear, dear friends."

She felt Mica's arms release her, and she wondered if her Flame was as disgusted with her as she felt with herself.

He sat down on the pillows in front of her, and lifted her chin so that he could look her in the eye.

"Emerald, my sweet Flame. You know as well as I do, that there is no such thing as separation. Whether we are with our Flame or not, we feel their presence as surely as if they are right next to us. I know that on Earth they still believe it is possible to be separate, to lose someone, and therefore to miss someone. But as painful as it is, you also know how necessary it is for them to sometimes feel that illusion of separation, to inspire them to fulfil their greatest missions yet."

Emerald bit her lip. "But look what happened last time. Velvet went home to the stars because the pain of losing him was too much. And look at us! You couldn't bear to stay there and continue your mission, you came home too."

"Velvet is so much stronger now. You know that. You have seen her cope with the loss of us from her life, and you have watched her help so many Flames cope with their own separations. She is not the same woman who left the Earth all those years ago."

"I guess so," Emerald said. "I just fear that we might be changing things for the worse, not for the better. Benit said himself that we have no way of really knowing. All we can do is to trust our intuition on what is the right choice."

Mica wiped away her tears with his handkerchief. "Benit is a wise Angel, listen to him. He has been doing this for a while."

Emerald nodded and smiled at her Flame. "I love you, Mica. I'm sorry I sometimes doubt myself."

Mica leaned forward to kiss her. "Your apologies are not needed. I know how deeply you feel the pain of others. And what we're doing does go against all we have been trained to believe here in the Angelic Realm. But I know, deep in my soul, that it is truly for the higher good of all. I trust Aragonite, and I also trust Starlight."

"Me too," Emerald agreed.

"Shall we get back to work?" Mica asked, holding his hand out to her. Emerald took it, and their wings lifted them to their feet, and they returned to their stations.

Chapter Six

Sleep was not forthcoming for Greg that night. He replayed the moment Violet had returned from the river in tears, their desperate salty kiss, and then the resulting conversation, over and over in his mind, wondering if he had made a colossal mistake, or whether it really was the best thing for the both of them.

He listened to Violet's breathing, and gripped her body just a little tighter to his. She sighed in her sleep and he felt a tear form and fall from the corner of his eye.

He had felt for a while that this moment would come, that they would need to part ways, not because they had fallen out of love, or because they hated each other, or because either of them had found someone else.

But because it was the right thing for their soul missions.

He breathed in Violet's scent, and wondered how he would be able to live without hearing her laugh, touching her skin, and kissing her until they both ran out of breath.

Not for the first time, he wished that he could just be a regular guy, living a normal life, working in an ordinary job, with a woman that he could share the ordinariness with.

But that was what he'd had in his old life, and look at how that had turned out.

He sighed softly and wondered if he should give up on sleep

and go and do something useful. But he knew that his nights of holding Violet in his arms were numbered, and somehow, he just couldn't let go just yet.

He closed his eyes, and wished he could just stay in that moment forever.

*   *   *

Gold had resisted for as long as he could, but while the Indigo Child was visiting her friends, and there appeared to be no one arriving imminently into the mists, he decided it would be a good time to see if Starlight had anything else to say to him.

He waved his hand in the mist, creating a swirl that he then dropped a shimmering pink drop into. Seconds later, he was looking into the eyes of his true love.

"Gold," she said, a smile on her face. "My love. I know you miss me desperately, but if you heed my message, there really is no need to. You could see me again very soon."

Gold nodded. "But I'm so afraid, what if it doesn't work out? What if me leaving here affects the timeline negatively? Oh, I wish you were really here to answer my questions."

"The answers you seek are within you, my love," Starlight said, eerily replying to his words. "You need not seek the answers outside of yourself. You know that, you have been saying so for as long as I have known you."

Gold sighed. He could sense someone approaching, and he didn't want to explain what he was going. He whispered goodbye and waved his hand. Starlight disappeared into the pink mists, and a second later, a soul appeared before him.

"Who are you? Where am I? I don't understand. A moment ago I was asleep in my bed, and now I'm here. I must be dreaming, but this… this feels too real to be a dream."

Gold patiently waited for them to pause in their dialogue, before beginning to explain.

"My child, you are currently in the mists between the third dimension and the fifth. While you slept, there was a gas leak, and you have breathed in too much of it, causing your soul to leave your body. You now have a choice to make. Do you wish to stay?"

"Stay? Where? Here or on Earth?"

"Here. The Other Side. You can stay here, move on to your next journey, wherever that may lead. Or you can return to Earth."

The soul frowned. "But you just said I was dead from a gas leak. How can I go back? Surely there's no coming back from that?"

Gold tilted his head. "If you chose to go back, we can arrange for someone to raise the alarm, for you to be rescued just in time."

"Oh. I see." The soul was quiet for a while, and Gold felt impatient for them to make their choice. He needed to go and visit Pearl, and ask for her counsel regarding his possible return to Earth.

"I think I would like to go back. I remember my previous lives now. I know I am an Awakened Human, I went to the classes here at the Academy that Linen and Aria created. But I hadn't woken up properly, I wasn't doing as I had intended to do. I would like another chance."

Gold nodded. "Very well. We will make sure you are rescued and you recover from this incident."

The soul smiled. "Thank you. What do I do now?"

"Just return from where you came, your Guardian Angel will guide you back over."

"Thank you, I'll see you again."

"Yes, perhaps." Gold watched the soul disappear into the mists, and sighed. It had seemed so easy for the soul to make the decision to return to Earth. As though there really wasn't much to consider. Yet Gold felt very torn on what he should do himself.

"I'm back, Gold, you may go to see Pearl now."

Gold turned to see the Indigo Child approaching, and he frowned. "How did you?" He shook his head. "Never mind. Thank you, I will be back shortly."

"Of course," the Child replied. "Take as long as you need."

Gold nodded and headed into the mists to the gates to the Angelic Realm, where he knew his trusted Angel friend would be.

*   *   *

"I think Julie should move into the spare room in the house with the kids, and work here full time doing the retreats. Lisa would be happy to host them, and Beatrice would probably pitch in too, now that she's more local."

Greg blinked at Violet sleepily, who was sat at the breakfast counter, paper spread out everywhere before her, a cup of tea in hand.

She glanced up when he didn't reply, and smiled sadly. "Morning. I was awake early, didn't want to disturb you."

"Morning," Greg replied, rubbing the sleep from his eyes. It had taken him an age to finally fall asleep, by which time it had started to get light. He went over to the kettle and made himself a strong coffee, and a fresh tea for Violet.

He brought them over to where she sat and he glanced at the organised chaos before her.

"Run all that by me once more?"

Violet repeated her words, slower this time, and Greg's tired, befuddled brain managed to comprehend them this time.

"You think I should still run the Twin Flame Retreats? Even though we're..."

Violet sighed and looked at him. He could see the sadness in her eyes, despite her cheery attitude. "I know it seems weird, but honestly I think it's even more important to hold them. Souls going through this situation need help. It's really not very easy."

Greg frowned. "So why are you trying to make it look like it is?"

Violet pursed her lips together and Greg saw her eyes begin to fill with tears. "Because what else can I do? If I stop for too long to think about what we're about to do, I will just crumble into a heap and not move for several months. I keep getting flashbacks to last time, and honestly, I just can't cope with it being like that again. I need to get through this as positively as possible."

Greg nodded. He knew she was making sense, but his heart felt incredibly heavy too. "What do I need to do?"

Violet shrugged. "Keep doing the retreats, while working out what you really enjoy doing. I know that you have an important purpose on this Earth, as do I, it's just finding it, or even deciding upon it."

"You really believe we can just choose a purpose, just pick one from a list?"

Violet sighed. "It's better than waiting for your purpose to fall out of the sky and into your lap, don't you think? After all, if you pick something and it doesn't work out or fit, you could just pick something else."

Greg sipped his coffee. "Yeah, I guess. I'm going outside."

"Aren't you going to eat anything? I made pancakes."

Greg stood up and shook his head. His stomach churned at the idea of eating anything. He moved toward Violet to kiss her before leaving, then remembered that they were breaking up, paused for a moment, then left the kitchen and headed outside, shoving his feet into his boots along the way.

He stepped outside the front door, and breathed in the cool, fresh scent of the trees and grass. He had intended to go to his workshop and continue working on his projects, but instead he found himself walking down the path to the bench by the pond. He sat down and sipped his coffee while staring at the unmoving water.

It felt as though Violet was taking the whole thing in her stride, that their separation was not a big deal. Though his memories were hazy, he had this heavy feeling left over from the moment of clarity he'd had in La Rochelle, when he'd realised that he had been a fool to push Violet away, and that they needed to be together. The heaviness had lingered all these years, and he felt it more clearly now. It was a feeling that if they parted again, it could be a very long time before he held her in his arms again.

Greg heard a rustling sound and looked up, expecting to see a deer on the path. He was surprised when he saw Lisa standing there.

"Hey," he said. "I didn't hear the car come up."

"Sorry I disturbed you. Couldn't figure out if you were meditating or just sitting very still."

Greg chuckled. "Just thinking. What's up?"

Lisa tilted her head to one side. "Violet asked to me to come over, said she had something to ask me. What's going on? You look terrible and she didn't sound right."

Greg sighed. It was difficult to hide things from people who were intuitive. He patted the bench next to him. "Come sit for a moment."

Lisa frowned, but came over to the bench and sat down.

"We're separating," Greg said. "And when she leaves, Violet wants you to run the retreats with me, Julie, Amy and Beatrice."

Lisa's eyes widened and she shook her head. "What? Why? What happened?"

"Nothing really," Greg said. "We both just knew that we need some time apart. Space to really figure out what we want."

Lisa looked toward the house. "And Violet is okay with this? I mean, after last time..."

"I didn't realise you knew about that," Greg said. He hated anyone knowing about the time they had split up before. He felt so awful about it.

"Violet's mentioned it, and Amy. It sounded... terrible," Lisa said. She turned to Greg and he forced himself to meet her eyes.

"Is this because of what happened in Atlantis?" she asked, referring to the healing work she had done with both Greg and Violet a few years before. "You two are incredible together, your combined energy and power is what the world needs right now. Separating feels... wrong."

Greg sighed and looked back at the pond. "I don't know if it's related to Atlantis, I haven't really explored the idea. It only really happened yesterday."

"Yesterday! And Violet is organising who is taking over from her already?"

"I think she felt it too. She felt the need for us both to have some space. She's coping with it all a bit too well. I'm glad you've come over to talk to her."

Greg stood up and tipped the dregs of his coffee onto the soil.

"You don't want me to convince her to stay?" Lisa asked softly.

Greg's heart skipped a beat, and he wondered if it could be that easy, to get her to just stay there with him forever. Aware that Lisa was watching him intently, he forced himself to shake his head.

"No, thank you. I think this is for the best." He left Lisa sitting on the bench and headed to his workshop, determined to make some headway with the shelving he was building for one of the pods.

Once safely inside his workshop, Greg slumped back against the closed door, and knowing that no one would be able to see him, he allowed his tears to fall.

*   *   *

"Your actions have interfered with ours," Tanzanite said to Emerald.

She looked up at the Angel, as did several others in the Twin Flame Team, and frowned. "I'm sorry, what do you mean?"

Tanzanite sat next to Emerald and lowered his voice a fraction. "The Atlantis team had been working on getting a group of people to realise their ability to create matter in the same way they did in Atlantis. We got the information to them, they acted upon it, but before they could truly use the information in the way it was intended, to help change their paths, you split them up."

Emerald winced. "Velvet and Laguz are in the group, aren't they?"

"Yes, they and a couple of the others are originally from Atlantis, and their combined energy could make it possible to create matter from nothing. But that won't happen now because Velvet and Laguz are headed in opposite directions."

Emerald sighed. Perhaps her intuition had been wrong, perhaps she wasn't meant to separate them. "I'm sorry, I had no idea that it would affect your team's operation."

"Don't apologise, Angel," Benit interrupted. "All of our actions here have the possibility of interfering with one another, and there was bound to be clashes in action between teams when it concerns the Angel of Fate. There is nothing to apologise for, we are all doing what we feel is necessary." Benit turned to Tanzanite. "I am sure that the separation will not be for long, and who knows, perhaps it is the realisation of their manifesting abilities that brings them back together."

Tanzanite frowned, but Emerald could see his frustration dissipating, and she breathed a little easier.

"Maybe. It has just taken us some time to get that information through, and we really think it could have helped."

"It still will," Benit said. "Of that I have no doubt."

Tanzanite nodded and stood up. "I apologise for the interruption. Please resume as you were."

Emerald watched Tanzanite return to his station, and she smiled at Benit. "Thank you. But how can you be so sure that what I did was right?"

Benit smiled back. "Because sometimes, what feels most wrong, is the best thing for all concerned. You will see."

Emerald nodded, but her heart still felt heavy. She looked down at the water before her, and saw the pain on her friend's faces. She prayed silently to the Universe that they would not be separated for long.

*   *   *

"I know this has all happened really fast, but I think it's all worked out for the best."

Greg swallowed hard, but nodded. He looked into Violet's eyes, and struggled to find the right words to say.

A tear slid down Violet's cheek, and he knew she was having the same trouble.

Amy was staying a respectful distance away, down by her campervan that was filled with the things that Violet had wanted to take with her. It had only been a week since they had agreed to separate, and Violet had made all the necessary arrangements with such speed it had left Greg's head spinning.

"I've written everything down that you need to know, but if you need anything, you can just email me."

Greg nodded, but his heart ached. Going from sharing a bed, meals, a home, and work with this woman, to exchanging courteous emails felt too difficult to bear.

"I know," Violet whispered, stepping closer to him and wrapping her arms around his middle. He automatically wrapped his arms around her and bowed his head to breathe in the scent of her hair.

"I love you," he whispered, hoping that it was the right thing to say.

"I love you too," Violet replied.

He squeezed her tight, then forced himself to release her. Before she could step away he lifted her chin and stole one last kiss.

When Violet pulled away, Greg could feel her body trembling. She turned away quickly and walked down the driveway to where Amy was waiting. She got into the campervan and Amy waved to Greg before getting into the driver's side. Greg stood there and watched until the vehicle disappeared into the trees, and only moved when he felt a hand on his arm.

"Come inside," Julie said.

He nodded and followed her into the house, feeling like he had aged ten years in the last ten minutes. Once he was sat at the breakfast bar with a cup of hot, sweet tea in his hands, he managed to speak.

"Where has she gone?"

Julie frowned. "She didn't tell you?"

Greg shook his head. "No, and I didn't ask. I didn't feel like I had the right to know."

"She's going to see her parents, then she's flying to Canada before going to America. She has a few contacts there, she's going to see about getting her book out to a wider audience. I think she's going to do some talks, and attend some conferences."

"Wow, that's amazing," Greg said, feeling both pride in his wife and a deep sadness that he hadn't been able to hear the news from her. He frowned as the thought of finances crossed his mind. They'd had no savings, how was Violet affording to travel to America?

Julie smiled. "She's going to do well. She just needs to remember who she really is, and step fully into that role. Her parents are helping to fund the tour, I think she's hoping that it will result in more sales, and more exposure."

"That really is amazing," Greg said, wondering if his thoughts were written that plainly on his face.

They drank in silence for a moment, then Julie reached over to touch his arm.

"She still loves you, you know. It may seem like she left suddenly, and is off to do amazing things, but you need to know that it was tearing her to shreds inside."

Greg nodded, doing his best not to allow himself to break down in front of his friend. "I know. I hope she knows that I feel the same way."

"I know she does. She feels everything you feel, she's so in tune with your energy."

Greg said nothing for a few moments, but then he felt he just had to say his thoughts out loud. "Have I made a terrible mistake, Julie? Should I have stopped her from leaving?"

Julie was quiet for a while, but finally, she shook her head. "No, I think this was the right thing for both of you. And that though it feels shitty right now, it will be perfect at some point in the future."

Greg tried to smile. "Thanks."

Julie patted his arm again. "I better go check on the kids, hopefully they're still watching the movie. Are you sure it's okay to be staying in the house? I know that Violet arranged it all, not you."

"Of course it's okay, it's good to have some company. Besides it's a little more comfortable than the pods."

Julie nodded, then went upstairs to check on her children. Greg went over to the kettle to make himself another cup of tea. While waiting for the water to boil, he looked at the calendar and saw Violet's loopy script covering it, reminders of all the things he now needed to take care of.

He flipped through it, and saw that she had written on every month for the rest of the year. Which meant that she didn't plan to return for at least the next eight months.

Greg bowed his head and prayed that they would one day be together again, and that eleven years was not all he was allowed to have with his Flame in this lifetime.

A tear fell and hit the counter. Greg took a deep breath, vowed to find out what his mission was, and focus on that while Violet focussed on hers.

So that when they met again, he would be ready to spend the rest of his days with her.

Chapter Seven

"Galena, may I have a word?" Pearl asked as she approached her good friend who was sat on the pebbles at the edge of the lake. The Angel looked up and smiled.

"Of course, what is it?" she asked, rising gracefully to her feet. She joined Pearl and they walked away from earshot of the other Angels nearby.

"I have been hearing rumours at the gate, that there is a team of Angels working on changing the current timeline. Do you know of this?"

Galena blushed a little. "Yes, I have heard the rumours."

"Are they true? Because Gold does not seem to know about it, nor Pallas, and I don't know of anyone else here with the authority to orchestrate such a team. If there is a full-scale rebellion happening, I need to know."

Galena was quiet for a moment. "Are you trying to stop them? Because as far as I can see, they aren't doing anything different to what we were doing while on Earth in human form. In fact, I believe it was our mission that created a shift big enough to spark this whole new mission."

Pearl stopped walking and turned to the Angel. "What do you mean?"

Galena stopped too. "When you stopped the explosion, and there was no damage done to the buildings, and no lives were lost, it was hailed as a miracle. Instead of fear being borne of that event, hope and faith were created instead. The subtle shift in energy meant that a ripple effect has been created. And with the help of this new team of Angels, the Golden Age is more than just a possibility, it is a certainty."

Pearl didn't know how to respond. She had only just dealt with her own fears that they had messed with the timeline due to their actions on Earth, and though it seemed as though they had created a positive ripple, and they had steered the world in a brighter direction, it still worried her that they had been able to do it.

It seemed like too much power for the Angels to possess.

"Our team was controlled and regulated by Pallas and the Elders. Who is regulating this new team? And please, who started it?"

Galena sighed and began walking again. "I don't know who started it, but I believe an Angel called Aragonite is the one coordinating it. I sent two Angels to speak with him not long ago, and they did not come back to me, so I assume the information was correct." She glanced sideways at Pearl. "Are you going to report it and shut it down?"

Pearl frowned. "I'm unsure at this moment in time. Condoning it may inspire other Angels to rebel, and start nudging the humans in a manner that is not for the highest good of all. I will need to speak with Aragonite, and then decide. It does appear that there are a great many changes afoot, and I wish to keep abreast of them all."

"What other changes are happening?" Galena asked.

Pearl sighed. She knew that telling Galena was probably not the best idea, seeing as she appeared to have trouble keeping information to herself, but then she also figured that word would spread soon enough.

"Gold is considering going to Earth to fulfil the prophecies."

Galena gasped. "Really? But that hasn't happened in millennia."

"I know. At the moment, his decision is not set. But considering how keen he is to see Starlight, I cannot imagine he will be able to turn down the opportunity."

"How will we cope here without him? I mean, Velvet is there, Starlight is there, as is Athena, and your Flame. Soon, there will be more Elders on Earth than on the Other Side."

"Perhaps that is the only way we can save the humans from their most likely demise," Pearl mused. "Anyway, it is not certain yet, so I would appreciate you keeping it to yourself."

Galena nodded, but Pearl could tell that the request was lost on her.

She sighed. "I should return to my post and relieve Opalite. I will seek out Aragonite. Thank you for the information."

"Please, don't mention that I told you to go there, I don't wish for him to distrust me."

Pearl smiled. "Of course." They embraced, and then Pearl set off back toward the gates, to where Opalite stood on duty.

She had no idea what was going on in the Angelic Realm, but she was determined to find out.

*   *   *

Violet folded her clothes as small as possible, and tucked them into her suitcase. She planned to travel around Canada and America for several weeks, and wanted to pack light. She would be carrying her luggage around a lot.

"How's it going?"

Violet smiled at her mother. "It's going fine. Thanks for letting me store some stuff here while I'm away. I wasn't sure what I might need or want."

"Of course." Her mother frowned. "Are you sure this is what you want? It all seems so sudden."

Violet looked down at her wedding ring, and twisted it around her finger. She wished her mother wouldn't be so sympathetic, it made it hard to remain stoic about her decision.

"It's the right thing for us both," she said, hating that her voice wavered, giving her away.

Her mother stepped toward her and wrapped her in a comforting, familiar hug. "It doesn't mean it doesn't hurt though," she whispered into Violet's ear.

The tears began to fall, and Violet was powerless to hold them back. Her mother held her until she managed to calm down, and then kissed her on the forehead. "I will support you no matter what you decide. But it's not too late to go back to him."

Violet sighed and blew her nose. She nodded and her mother left the room. Violet sat down heavily on her childhood bed and sighed. She had been fighting the urge to run back to the forest, back to Greg, since the moment Amy had dropped her off at her parents' house. She missed him with every part of her body and soul.

But she had this weird inner nudge that was making her want to spread her wings, and interact with a larger audience. In a very short space of time, just two weeks, she had managed to arrange flights, accommodation, and speaking gigs at several events. One of them was a really big conference and somehow, at the last minute, they'd had someone cancel, so there was a space for her.

It had all been effortless, easy, and therefore, Violet knew that it was the right path to take.

Even if her heart did still hurt.

Three days later, Amy picked her up, and drove her to the airport. They'd listened to the radio the whole way there, Violet had the feeling that her friend was struggling to speak. When they arrived outside departures, Amy turned to her.

"Are you sure about this?"

Violet smiled at her friend. "Yes. I need to do this. I know that if I don't, I will always wonder what might have been, and neither me nor Greg could live with that. Even if nothing comes of it, I need to find out."

Amy nodded. "I'll miss you. But I know you'll be awesome. Do you want me to keep you updated on what's happening at the Retreat?"

Violet thought for a moment, then shook her head. "No, I think it's better to not know what's going on. Unless there's something you need my help with, of course. I think I need to just focus on my writing and speaking, and see what happens next."

"Are you keeping in touch with Greg while you're away?"

Violet shook her head again. "No, I'm going to give him some space. He needs to focus as much as I do. It won't be easy, but I think it's important."

Amy didn't look convinced, but didn't say anything further.

"Thank you, Angel, for being there for me. And for bringing me to the airport. I appreciate it."

"Of course," Amy said, wrapping her arms around Violet awkwardly across the seats of the campervan. "Let me know when you've landed safely, okay?"

"Sure." Violet pulled away, and before the tears could start, she got out of the van and grabbed her small suitcase from the back. She ignored the pointed glares of the security people who obviously hated long farewells and she waved to her friend one last time before stepping through the automatic doors and into the airport. She paused for a moment, taking in the sight of people rushing around, checking in for flights, and then took a deep breath and set off to begin her next new adventure.

* * *

Greg was aware of the animated conversation going on around him, but was unable to focus on the individual words in order to keep up with the four women. It wasn't until there was a lull in the chatter that he looked around to realise that they were all looking at him.

"Are you okay?" Julie asked softly, putting her hand on his arm. "We could have this meeting another time, only Beatrice was able to get a sitter and the next retreat is only a week away, so we really need to figure out who will be doing what and what preparation is needed."

Greg shook his head, then nodded. "I'm okay. Sorry, I zoned out a little. I haven't been sleeping all that well. Could you just run through what you were all saying again?"

Lisa smiled at him. "Your role will be the same as usual, doing the emotional release work, and then working with the men separately to the women for one of the workshops. And then when it comes to food, Beatrice will be helping you with that, and Amy will be on pod and clean up duty. I'll do the workshops that Violet would usually do, and Julie will be coordinating the schedule and making sure everyone has everything they need, as well as doing the evening activities."

Greg nodded. "Okay, I got all that this time. It sounds good."

"Of course, we'll all pitch in wherever we're needed, but if we have our individual roles, at least nothing will get missed out," Beatrice said.

"It sounds like you all have everything under control, I'll do my best to keep up."

"It will be fine. Violet gave me access to the website and emails, so I have been keeping on top of the bookings. The participants know that she won't be here, but they seem happy enough that it's being run by us."

"They didn't find it ironic that the Twin Flame Retreat is now being run by a separated Flame?"

"Greg, many of them have been in the exact same place. They understand," Amy said. "It's not unusual for Flames to separate, you know that."

Greg nodded. "I promise I will do my best to be my usual self by the retreat. I'm just finding it a little difficult to adjust right now."

"That's understandable."

A moment later, Charlotte came running into the room, crying, and Julie got up to go and tell Dan off for being mean to her. Beatrice looked at her watch.

"I have to go, my sitter could only give me two hours. I'll see you all soon."

"I'll come out with you," Amy said, getting to her feet. "Got an early start tomorrow."

The two women gave Greg a hug, then left.

Lisa looked over to Greg. "Would you like some healing? I can't even begin to imagine how hard the last couple of weeks have been, and I would like to help ease that, if I can."

Greg sighed. "That would be good, thank you."

Lisa smiled and motioned for him to lay down on the giant

cushions scattered on the floor in the workshop room where they were sat. He complied, and tucked a soft pillow under his head. Lisa knelt next to him, and he closed his eyes.

He could sense the heat coming from her hands held over his head. He breathed deeply, getting himself into a calm state. He focussed on his breath, and did his best to let go of all the thoughts running wild in his mind. After a few moments, he could see an image rushing toward him, until suddenly, he found himself within a memory, one that he had long forgotten.

"Laguz?"

Hearing his name float toward him in the water was the strangest experience, and Laguz didn't think he would ever get used to it. He smiled at Lacy as she swam toward him, but it appeared as more of a grimace.

"We need to hold counsel with the other Mer-Elders. There is discord among them over how this new underwater realm should be organised, and many are becoming fearful that we will fall into mutiny. You must call a meeting, and step into the role that Velvet foresaw for you."

Laguz sighed. In Atlantis, he had held a position of authority, but never had to step up in this way. His people, now Merpeople, were depending on him to create a whole new world, a whole new paradigm, under the water, and he had no idea how to do it.

"We can do it together," Lacy said, appearing to sense his thoughts. "I know you are mourning the loss of your Flame, we are all missing Velvet, but our people live on, and we must help them to adjust to this new, strange world we find ourselves in."

Laguz took a deep breath of water, and nodded. He straightened up from where he had slumped among the rocks, and swam gracefully to where Lacy hovered.

She smiled at him and took his hand. "You're not alone, I'm right here."

Greg felt a small, warm hand in his, and it brought him out of his vision and back into the workshop room at the Twin Flame Retreat. He opened his eyes and looked up at Lisa, who had tears in her eyes.

"You saw that too," he said, feeling more deeply connected

to the Old Soul than he ever had before.

She nodded. "It's the first time I have seen a memory of our underwater existence. It seems we must have worked together then, too."

Greg sat up slowly, her hand still in his. "I'm very lucky to have such strong Earth Angels around me, helping me right now. Though Violet is only separated from me by distance, not death, I still feel as though I am grieving. I don't think it would be as easy to deal with if you, Julie, Amy and Beatrice weren't here to help me."

Lisa smiled, and Greg reached out to wipe away her tear. He realised too late that the action was quite an intimate one, and he took his hand away when he realised their close proximity, and her sweet, floral scent.

She shifted uncomfortably and pulled her hand away from his, clearly sensing his feelings. "I need to go, Missy will be hungry. I hope the healing helps." She got up quickly, and though Greg knew it was the right thing for her to do, he missed the warmth of her hand in his. He listened to her go downstairs and out the front door, and then lay back down on the cushions. He could hear Julie and the kids in the spare room, and an owl hooting outside.

He closed his eyes, and allowed himself to grieve.

* * *

"Was it a good idea to give them that memory?"
"They helped each other through tough times before, they can do the same thing again."

"That may be, but don't you remember exactly what happened last time?"

Emerald frowned at the conversation she was overhearing from the Atlantis Team. What memory had they given who?

Tanzanite noticed her and raised his eyebrows. "Can we help you, Emerald?"

The Angel blushed, wondering if they knew she had been listening.

"I came over to see if it you thought it would be a good

idea to perhaps have some meetings, you know, between the different teams. Because it seems as though our nudges may end up conflicting with one another. Because I really had no idea that my actions would nullify yours."

Tanzanite frowned, and Emerald could tell that he was having trouble believing her. She wondered why the Angel had become so distrusting and cynical.

"If you don't think it would be beneficial, that's okay," she said, holding up her hands and backing away from them.

"No, wait, I think it's a good idea," an Angel called Olivine said. "There's little point in us trying to influence a person or situation if it's going to clash with something that you are doing."

"What's going on?"

The Angels all looked up to see Aragonite standing there, clearly wondering why they were sitting around chatting rather than nudging their human charges.

"We were talking about having meetings between the teams, so that our nudges don't cancel each other out," Emerald explained, feeling a little bolder now that she had the support of Olivine.

Aragonite nodded. "It could be a good idea. Perhaps each team could choose a representative and then those Angels could have meetings to discuss their strategies."

Everyone nodded except for Tanzanite, who still looked a bit sullen.

"Excellent, I will announce it at the next bigger picture showing, which will be later on today."

"Already?" Emerald asked. "Do you think we will be able to see much of a change in the timeline? It's only been a few weeks."

"It might not have been a very long time, but some of the key Earth Angels have gone through some big changes, so yes, I believe it will be possible to see a change. And I think it's important, now that we have the capability to, to keep up-to-date with the changes as they happen, so we can adjust our actions accordingly."

Emerald nodded. She could see his point. Aragonite went on

his rounds, and Emerald said goodbye to the Atlantis Team. She returned to her station and explained to Mica and Benit what had just transpired.

"I do think that working together as a whole will make the shift happen so much easier," Mica said. "But what memory do you think they were talking about?"

Emerald shook her head. "I don't know, but it sounded important. Keep an ear out to see if anyone mentions it within the Twin Flame Retreat. Because I would bet anything that it had something to do with one of them."

"Will do," Benit said. "I'm looking forward to seeing the big picture again, do you really think it might have changed?"

Emerald shrugged. "I have no idea. I guess we'll find out."

A short while later, the call went out for the Angels to gather to see the bigger picture.

Emerald and Mica sat side by side, and watched the bigger picture unfold, but instead of the elation she had expected to feel, fear and horror built up until the final crescendo.

Chapter Eight

"Welcome!"

Violet blinked sleepily and squinted at the lady with a beaming smile waiting at the airport arrivals area. "Saphron?"

"No, I'm Vivi, Saphron's friend, she's parking the car. Here, let me take this," Vivi said, taking Violet's case from her. They fell into step and set off toward the exit.

"Sorry, it was a very bumpy flight and I'm feeling quite tired," Violet said.

"That's cool, I'm just so excited to meet you. Saphron and I have read your book and we love it! We're so thrilled to be able to spend some time with you on your trip."

Violet smiled; the woman's enthusiasm was lifting her energy already. "That's wonderful. I look forward to spending time with you both too."

They went outside and Violet saw a blur of orange as Saphron rushed up to her and hugged her.

"Oh!" she gasped. "Hello, Angel!"

Saphron squeezed her hard then pulled away, her face glowing.

"Violet! I'm so pleased to meet you!"

Violet chuckled. "Likewise! I feel quite at home here already, thank you both, beautiful Angels."

They went to the car which was parked in the drop off

zone, loaded Violet's case and then set off through the city to Saphron's home by the lake.

"I'm so pleased you decided to start your trip in Canada before heading to the States," Saphron said. "I have been wanting to meet you and talk to you properly since I read your book."

"It seemed to make sense," Violet said. "There's the big Angel Conference happening here, which I managed to get a speaking gig at, and flights were cheaper to Canada, so I thought – why not?"

The three women chatted about the Angel Conference for the rest of the short journey, as Vivi and Saphron were also planning to attend. Once they were seated in Saphron's sitting room with a fresh pot of fruit tea, Saphron leaned toward Violet.

"I know who I am," she said, excitement shining on her face.

Violet frowned and looked at her new friend. "What do you mean?"

"From the Academy. I read your book and I recognised myself in it."

Violet smiled. "You did? That's great. I've met many of the souls from the Academy already. Who are you?"

"Chiffon. Professor of Manifestation."

Violet's eyebrows shot up and she took in the energy and appearance of the woman before her and she nodded her head. Of course. It was so obvious now that she had pointed it out. "Oh, Saphron! Yes, I can see that now." Violet set her cup of tea down and the two women embraced. Violet felt quite emotional at meeting yet another of the professors who had come to Earth to support her in her mission of Awakening others.

"Thank you for coming back to Earth," Violet whispered.

Saphron pulled back and smiled. "It hasn't been the easiest thing I've ever done, but I'm glad I did. This is the most important mission of our existence. I couldn't let you come back alone."

Violet felt tears filling her eyes. "Thank you, Angel."

"So when is the next book coming out? Are you going to write about the Earth Angels on Earth? About their missions? About the Flames? You've met your Flame, right? I want to know if I'm going to meet mine, do you do readings?"

Violet laughed at the stream of questions from Vivi. "I'm sure we can arrange a reading, but right now I am a bit wiped out. I may need to get some sleep."

"Of course, your room is upstairs on the left. We can talk more tomorrow."

Violet nodded in appreciation, picked up her case from the hallway and went upstairs. Once she was underneath the covers in the bed in Saphron's spare room, the physical distance between her and Greg sank in, and she cried until she fell into a dreamless sleep.

*   *   *

Pearl watched the bigger picture unfold on the swirling screen of mist in front of her, her eyes wide and her heart pounding.

How was this possible? The only way they could have access to the bigger picture was through Starlight, but she was on Earth, not on the Other Side.

She watched the events unfold, and noted all the differences to the old timeline. She wondered how much of it would have happened naturally as a result of Velvet's return, and how much of it was as a result of her team's interference on Earth, and the interference of this gathering of Angels in front of her.

Pearl returned her attention to the water, and was horrified to see events taking a turn for the worse, and the world ending in chaos and darkness.

As soon as the vision disappeared, the Angels in front of her erupted into chatter.

"Was it us? What did we do wrong?" one Angel called out.

"What can we do? We cannot let this happen!" another cried.

Aragonite stepped up to the front of the room, his face ashen. He calmed the terrified Angels quickly, then spoke.

"We cannot know what our work here will do on Earth. We have known that from the beginning. This shift in events may be a result of our work, but equally it may have nothing to do with it. But at least, by seeing this, we can be ever more vigilant, and look out for positive shifts we can nudge the humans toward, to ensure that this potential bigger picture does not become the reality." He took a deep breath. "I have utter faith in you, do not despair now, just focus on keeping your vibration high and your intentions pure."

Pearl tuned out as he explained to the Angels about the introduction of inter-team meetings to discuss strategy. Soon, he dismissed them back to their stations.

Pearl waited for the chattering Angels to leave the room before she made her way over to the Angel with light brown wings.

"Aragonite," she said softly.

His head snapped in her direction and she saw a look of resignation flit across his face. "I didn't think it would take long for you to find us out," he said with a sigh.

"I just witnessed the bigger picture, and I think we need to talk."

Aragonite sighed. "It's not as bad as it appears. The first time we looked, the outcome was amazing, so much better than it was previously. I feel there are just some small tweaks we need to do, and it will all get back on track again."

"How can you be so sure?" Pearl asked. "You have no way of knowing what to tweak! You could make it worse. I'm not sure I can allow this rebellion to continue."

Aragonite frowned. "Rebellion? That's a little strong isn't it? I know you are against meddling with free will, but you yourself did as we are doing, only on Earth, in person."

Pearl sighed. "I know I did, and I struggle in every moment to justify my actions and my role in that. I have been told that by stopping the terrorist attack, I had a positive effect on the world, but I struggle to believe that too."

Aragonite nodded. "Yes, stopping the terrorist attack in the way you did was the catalyst for all of this. But there was something else, too, which has had a rather large impact."

Pearl frowned. "What was that?"

Aragonite motioned for her to follow him to his basin of water, away from the main teams of Angels. Pearl sat at the basin, and Aragonite waved his hand over it.

Pearl looked into the water, and watched a radiant young girl sitting in a cross legged position, meditating with a serene smile on her face. The girl looked familiar, but Pearl didn't know who she was.

"I don't understand," Pearl said to Aragonite. "Who is she?"

"Keep watching," Aragonite said gently.

Pearl looked back at the water, where time had skipped ahead, and the girl was now sitting next to a child, her hand on his, while she spoke softly.

"The Angels will heal you. You will be well enough to dance again. All will be well. Simply believe."

Pearl's eyes widened. She could see the healing energy flow from the girl to the small boy, and could see that she genuinely was healing him.

Another boy approached the two of them. When Pearl looked closely and saw his grey eyes, it all fell into place.

"She is the child I healed in hospital on Christmas Day," she whispered. "And that was the boy who saw me there. No one else saw me." She looked up at Aragonite, tears in her eyes. "She is now a healer? Spreading word of the Angels?"

Aragonite nodded. "Word of her own healing miracle has spread. And now she is also performing healing miracles herself."

Tears streamed down Pearl's cheeks as she watched the young girl as she went about her day. She could see some similarities now to the pale child who had lain dying. But the glow around her was visible, and the peace that emanated from her seemed to calm and heal all those in the vicinity.

"What effect did this have on the timeline?"

"It increased the belief in Angels, and therefore improved the communication between the Guardian Angels and their charges. The number of people healing from seemingly incurable diseases is also increasing because this little girl has given them hope, and faith in miracles again."

Pearl smiled and wiped her damp cheeks with her sleeve. "I never dreamed that saving one child's life could make such a difference to the world."

Aragonite smiled. "This is why we are doing this, because small changes make big differences. And saving a life is no small thing. Not to those who love her, and not to all those healed by her now." He sighed. "Please don't shut us down. I know we can get back on track to a more positive future, if you stop us now, though, we will have to just stand by and watch the world descend into darkness."

Pearl was quiet for a while, as she watched the young girl in the basin. "Was it you who started this mission? How did you get access to the bigger picture?"

Aragonite smiled. "I am not an Archangel or Elder, I would not have had the authority to do this off my own back. It was Starlight. We met while dealing with the rogue planets. She asked me to run a team of Angels here, to do what we did on those other planets. She gave the bigger picture to two Angels, Emerald and Mica, who brought it to me. It has been an invaluable tool to see if our actions are taking us in the right direction."

Pearl nodded. She had suspected that Starlight had to be involved. She was pleased to hear that the issues on the other planets had been solved. She still felt a bit apprehensive about allowing the Angels to continue meddling with free will, but Aragonite was right, if she stopped them now, the humans were doomed for certain. She got to her feet.

"How can I help you and your team?"

Aragonite sighed in relief. "You already have helped. You started it all. All we need is the grace to keep doing what we are doing. Perhaps you could grant us your protection from being stopped by the other Elders, or Pallas? At least until we get Earth back on course again?"

Pearl nodded. Though it went against her ingrained beliefs as an Angel, to rebel against the system, to disobey orders, she could see that her disobedience on Earth had actually paid off, and so, she would do it again.

"I will protect this mission, and make sure that word of it does not reach the Elders. I will inform Pallas and Gold that the rumours are simply that, just rumours. You have my grace."

Aragonite bowed his head. "Thank you. That will help us

so much."

"You're very welcome, Angel. I must return to my post now. I will set up the protection as I leave here. Please send an Angel with updates at regular intervals, I need to know that things on Earth are getting back on track, for my own peace of mind. You know where I am."

Aragonite nodded and reached out to embrace the Angel. "Of course, Pearl. I will do that."

She held him tightly for a moment, then released him. "Peace, love and light be with you always."

"And with you," he replied.

*   *   *

"What's it like? Being with Laguz again?"

Violet smiled at Saphron's use of Greg's soul name. "It's amazing. It's beautiful. It's challenging. It's at times heart-breaking and frustrating too. Like most relationships, I imagine." She hadn't told Saphron or Vivi that she and Greg were currently separated. It still felt too raw and painful to talk about.

Saphron shook her head and looked out at the water as they walked along the beach. "I've not met mine yet. I'm beginning to think that it just isn't going to happen in this life, despite all our plans."

"You met with your Flame before leaving the Academy?" Violet asked, bending down to pick up a pebble from the sand.

"Yes. We met before we incarnated this time, and we agreed to do our best to find each other. But he is so mission orientated, I feel he may have focussed more on his mission than he has on finding me."

Violet smoothed her thumb over the slightly rough surface of the pebble, and considered how she should respond. She didn't like to give spiritual platitudes to souls who could see right through them. She wanted to be able to speak the truth. "He is here still. He is single, he has never married. And you're right, his mission has been his sole focus, but..."

Saphron looked up at Violet and tilted her head to one side. "But?" she asked impatiently when the pause grew longer.

Violet looked back at the former Academy professor. "That will change. Very soon. There will be a wakeup call of some kind, and he will begin his search." Violet was amazed at how the words had flowed through her so effortlessly. She hoped that it was the truth, and not just her own wishes for her dear friend.

Saphron smiled brightly. "Wow, thank you. That means a lot to me. I was beginning to think it would just be me and Jasper forever," she said, referring to her white cat.

Violet smiled. "You have a wonderful life. You help people with your healing work and your radio show, and you have a beautiful home and feline friend. Not to mention many Earth Angel friends too."

Saphron nodded. "Yes, you're right, my life is amazing, and I am grateful for all the blessings in my life. Still can't help wishing for someone to share it all with. Who can talk back," she added, laughing.

"I can understand that," Violet said. "Before I met Greg, it always felt like my happiness was a little bit hollow, like there was a hole where another person needed to be. Not to complete me, but more just to add to the happiness, add to the joy." Violet shook her head. "I don't think I'm making much sense. For some reason, the journey here has caused me jet lag."

Saphron giggled. "The journey from the Fifth Dimension to Earth? Or from the UK to Canada?"

Violet laughed with her. "Both. My head feels like it's constantly spinning."

The two women walked along in silence for a while. The sun was out, but the breeze was quite cold and Violet shivered as it picked up and swirled around them.

"Do you miss the Academy? Miss running the place?"

Violet sighed. "Yes, I do."

"What do you miss most?"

Violet smiled. "I guess being able to make a difference. I had some authority there, a position that could help a lot of souls. Here, I feel..." Violet searched for the right word to describe how she felt in her human existence. "Powerless."

Saphron frowned. "Powerless? Really? But your book, your

story about the Academy, is powerful. Your retreats sound pretty powerful too."

"They are, you're right. And the written word is far more powerful than most humans realise. But I guess there is part of me that feels limited. By my body, my age and my experience in this lifetime. I also thought that things would be easier by now. A few years ago, I toured the UK doing talks and book signings, and the retreats have been going well, but royalties are still modest and we still struggle financially."

They walked further, passing a young woman with six dogs on leads. They skirted around her, trying not to get tangled up.

Violet broke the silence between them this time. "What are you thinking, dear soul?"

"You have forgotten again."

Violet frowned. "I have? What have I forgotten?"

"Who you really are. When we were at the Academy, the Children were arriving, the second years were turning up and suddenly everything shifted – it was clear then that there was much of your past you had forgotten. You had forgotten Laguz, your life in Atlantis, your powers to channel the energy of the Universe. You are a very powerful soul with the ability to create, or to manifest anything you could possibly dream of. And yet you are limiting yourself with the belief that you are the body you inhabit, that you are the sum of your experiences in this lifetime, and that you can only reach and help the people you can physically touch." Saphron stopped walking and Violet stopped too. The two women faced each other, and Saphron looked the Old Soul in the eye.

"Who are you?"

Violet frowned. "I'm Violet."

"Who are you?"

Violet raised an eyebrow at the repeated question. "I'm Velvet?"

"Who are you?"

"I'm a woman."

"Who are you?"

"I'm the former head of the Earth Angel Training Academy."

"Who are you?"

"I'm a Twin Flame."

"Who are you?"

The question was beginning to irritate Violet, so she answered sarcastically. "I am Velvet, Head of the Earth Angel Training Academy, the Angel of Fate, sister of Starlight, the Angel of Destiny and the Twin Flame of Laguz, the God of the Ocean, leader of the Merpeople."

Saphron smiled and nodded. "Yes, you are."

Violet laughed, her irritation gone. "It sounds like something from the *Lord of the Rings*."

"And yet every word of it is true," Saphron said, setting off down the path again.

"What does it matter though? If I start introducing myself like that to people, I'm going to get locked up."

Saphron giggled. "Probably. The important thing is that you know who you are, and that you act from that knowing. You don't have to tell anyone else. They will feel it through your words and actions anyway."

Violet breathed in deeply and considered her friend's words. As silly as it sounded, the words did make her stand a little taller, and feel a little more confident. "Who are you?" she asked Saphron.

Without a moment's hesitation, Saphron replied in her best Elven voice. "I am Orange Chiffon, Professor of Manifestation at the Earth Angel Training Academy, friend of Velvet, the Angel of Fate, former leader of the Elves of the Elemental Realm, Master Healer of DNA, Bringer of Light and Truth and Twin Flame of Sowilo, Master Engineer of Atlantis."

"I feel like I should curtsey!"

"No need," Saphron said, waving her hand dismissively. "A simple bow will do." She glanced sideways at Violet and they both started giggling.

Chapter Nine

Emerald looked around at the six other Angels, and was very pleased she had made this suggestion. They were each the elected team leaders who were now sharing the individual aims and missions of their teams.

Given the latest developments with the bigger picture, it seemed even more pertinent that they collaborate, in order to get Earth back on the more positive timeline they had witnessed before.

The Atlantis Team were focussed on helping people with inventions and innovations that would create alternative energy sources, and heal the planet of the damage the humans had already done. They were also focussed on manifestation, and the ability to create matter out of the nothingness.

"We feel that souls are still holding onto the belief that it takes time to invent, time to create things. That things don't just appear as a result of thought. The issue with this is that it's taking too long for things to be invented and created that will shift the world toward the Golden Age," Olivine said. "Therefore we are introducing, to some select souls who were in Atlantis, the memory that they were able to manifest things that did not already exist, and out of nothing more than the molecules in the air around them."

"Have any of them acted upon the information? Has it

worked?" an Angel from the Indigo Child Team asked.

"We gave the information to Lacy, who passed it onto Velvet and Laguz, and they brought a group together to try it, but when nothing materialised immediately, they didn't try it again."

"So they tried it, but it didn't work?" Another Angel asked.

"Actually," Olivine said. "It did work, it just materialised somewhere else."

Emerald was surprised. She had watched them try to manifest the dream recorder in the lake. "Where did it materialise?" she asked.

"In the lab of the person who was trying to invent exactly that. The invention will become public knowledge in the next couple of months, though we are trying to speed that up, because the faster that Velvet and her friends realise that they did in fact manifest such a thing, the quicker they will try the method again."

"So my nudge to split up Velvet and Laguz didn't ruin your work?" Emerald asked hopefully. She was fearful that their separation was the catalyst for the chaos and darkness they had witnessed earlier, and was in need of reassurance.

Olivine shook her head. "Don't mind Tanzanite. He can get a bit intense sometimes. You didn't ruin anything, it just worked out differently to how we originally imagined it might."

"You helped our work," an Angel called Tektite said. "Our team is working on increasing the belief in Angels. We needed Velvet to travel more, to speak more, and to become more well-known. If she and Laguz had not separated, then she wouldn't be about to speak in the world's largest Angel Conference, where she is headed right now. The ripple effect of her talk will make a huge difference."

"I was amazed that her plans to travel and speak fell into place so quickly and effortlessly," Emerald said. "I should have realised that angelic intervention was at play."

"Yes, what we managed to get into place for her in two weeks should have taken months to organise and prepare. But a fully coordinated sequence of nudges to the right people helped to bring it all together."

Emerald smiled. "That's good. As you know, the work of the

Twin Flame Team is to reunite the Flames, but we are finding that at the moment, it sometimes means separating them for short periods of time, so they have the space they need to heal their past life traumas. We feel that in order for the new timeline to flow easily toward the Golden Age, we need as many Twin Flames to be in harmonious unions as possible."

"The best way to ensure the reunion of the Flames is to make sure as many Earth Angels are Awake as possible," Labradorite said. "Our Awakening Team is doing just that. We are making sure that sleeping Earth Angels are receiving so many signs and moments of clarity that they cannot fail to Awaken faster. The more Awake they are, the more inner work they do, the more likely they are to be able to reunite with their Flame in a harmonious manner."

"How is the meeting going?"

The Angels all looked up to see Aragonite watching them.

"Good," Emerald offered. "It seems that even though we had not been aware of each other's missions, they are all complementing each other, regardless."

Aragonite nodded. "That's good, though I'm sure you will be able to work out even better strategies by working together. We need to ensure that we shift the world back onto the positive timeline. So try to work out where it is we may have gone wrong."

The Angels all nodded and murmured in agreement.

"Emerald, could you see me after? I have something I wish to ask you."

Emerald agreed, curious as to what information Aragonite could need from her. She tried to concentrate on the rest of the meeting, but found herself to be quite distracted. Was it to do with the changes in the timeline? Was she the one who had done something wrong?

When they finally wrapped up, with plenty of ideas to feed back to their teams, Emerald headed straight to where Aragonite sat, in front of his basin of water.

"What can I help you with?" she asked as she approached him.

Aragonite looked up at her. "As you are an expert in the area of Twin Flames, I wish to ask you whether you felt that I should reunite with mine."

Emerald's eyes widened. "With Blue Cotton?"

"Yes, my dear Blue. I visited her during a meditation, some time ago, when I was headed to the other planets. At the time, it was certain that I would not be returning, and that I would never get to experience a human life with my beautiful Flame. But things have changed. I know that my purpose has been to run this mission, but after seeing the timeline change for the worse, I am feeling a huge pull to go to Earth and reunite with my Flame, so we can have at least a few years together. It would mean leaving the mission in the hands of another Angel, and though I will try to wait until the bigger picture improves, the pull is really quite strong. I need to go to Earth to reunite with my Blue."

Emerald was quiet for a few moments, contemplating his question. Though she had not personally met Cotton on Earth, she had watched the Old Soul enough to know that she had been crushed when she discovered that she would not be with her Flame. But she also knew that she was currently following her mission, helping Earth Angels to make a living from their work, and assisting with the Twin Flame retreat. She wondered if being reunited with her Flame at this point would derail her from her mission, or if it would strengthen her and help her to shine even more brightly.

Then again, she could understand Aragonite's need to be with her, especially if the world continued on its current path.

Aware that Aragonite was waiting for her thoughts, Emerald looked deeply into the eyes of the Angel, and allowed herself to speak directly from her own heart.

"I believe that a reunion would be the best thing for you both," she began. Aragonite's face lit up, and then fell at her next words. "And the fact that you are willing to risk experiencing the darkness, assures me of your commitment to reuniting with her. But not yet. I do feel that you need to wait until the bigger picture improves, otherwise your fears for the future, and the future of your Flame, will harm your union." She reached out to touch his arm. "Be patient, hopefully it won't be too long."

"Can I tell her I am coming? Visit her in a dream or meditation?"

Emerald shook her head before she realised what she was doing. "No, she needs to continue on her current path for a while. The knowledge of your reunion will stop her from fully concentrating on her tasks." She smiled. "It will be a very welcome surprise, when you arrive on Earth."

Aragonite nodded, but Emerald could see that she hadn't delivered quite the message he had hoped for. She decided to leave, sensing his unspoken dismissal.

*   *   *

Greg was beginning to regret offering to take Daniel and Jerry shopping with him to get supplies for the retreat that weekend, while Julie and Charlotte cleaned the house. The two boys were in the cereal aisle, fighting over which cereal to get, and Greg could feel his patience wearing thin. He hated shopping at the best of times, but in the mood he was in, with two children in tow, he knew he could quite easily snap.

He pushed the trolley over to the two boys, took the two boxes out of their hands and threw them both into the trolley.

"Quit arguing, I need to concentrate," he said, trying to be gentle, but hearing the impatience in his own voice. The two boys looked a little shocked, having only ever seen his patient, kind side and both nodded and fell into line behind him, their bickering forgotten.

Greg grabbed some boxes of tea, and then a jar of honey. He had a list, but it seemed very short. Violet had always done the shopping for the retreats before. She always seemed to know what to get, what would be needed, and how to cater perfectly for her guests.

Much to his horror, tears began to fill his eyes. He would not let himself become emotional in the local supermarket, it would just be too horrifying.

"Uncle Greg? Are you okay? I think Mum said to get more biscuits," Daniel said, holding out a box to him. Greg rubbed his eyes and nodded.

"Yes, I'm fine, just tired. Thank you, biscuits are on the list. Why don't you two pick out some of your favourites too?"

The two boys grinned and then started eagerly scanning the shelves. Their attention diverted, Greg managed to wipe his eyes better with his sleeve. He needed to get himself together, the next retreat was starting in two days, and he needed to be on top form for it. Otherwise, he would be jeopardising his main income and ability to keep the Retreat going.

He wondered how Violet was doing, and where she was. Not having daily communication with her was one of the hardest things he'd ever had to do. Even harder than when they first split up, all those years ago.

He twisted his ring on his finger. There had been no discussion of divorce, or whether they would reunite in the future. He thought of his encounter with Lisa after the healing, and he felt guilt rising up.

In that vulnerable moment, he had felt close to her, felt an attraction to her. If it was possible for him to feel that way, then was Violet also attracting the attention of other men?

The thought of it made his stomach recoil. To distract himself, he motioned for the boys to add the several packets of biscuits to the trolley, then continued on with the shopping, trying to keep images of Violet with other men out of his mind.

Once they were finished in the supermarket, they loaded the bags into the van, and Greg felt the sudden urge to visit Ruby in the crystal shop. There was a crystal he needed to get for his healing treatments, and he also wanted to see if she was okay, as he hadn't seen her for a while.

The boys were happy to visit Ruby, she always let them choose a crystal from the treasure chest to keep.

They entered the small shop across the bridge, and Greg breathed in the familiar smell of incense.

He remembered the last time he'd been there, for his healing session with Lisa, when he found out why he and Violet were unable to conceive. He shook his head to himself. He wished that everything didn't remind him of Violet.

"Greg! How are you! It's been a long time!" Ruby came out from behind the counter and gave him a hug. His eyes widened at the sight of her, and she pulled away and grinned. She put her hand on her stomach. "My Flame returned, and well, we're about to have another Star Child." She frowned. "Didn't Lisa mention it?"

Greg shook his head and cleared his throat. "No, she didn't. Congratulations! On both accounts. I'm glad your Flame returned, and that you are expanding your family."

"Thanks, it's been a pretty crazy rollercoaster ride, but I wouldn't change it for the world. Would you like a cuppa?"

Greg shook his head. "I was actually looking for a crystal I needed, and we have shopping in the car, so we'll have to get going. We have another retreat this weekend."

Ruby waved at the poster behind the desk. "Yes, Julie sent me the poster, looks like a good one. Are you guys ready for it?"

Greg appreciated her not mentioning Violet being away. At that moment, he didn't think he could handle hearing her name.

"I think so, just finding a new way of doing things. Amy, Julie, Lisa and Beatrice have been amazing."

"Did I hear my name?"

Greg looked up to see Lisa emerging from the back room with a client behind her. He smiled and nodded. "I was just telling Ruby how amazing you were, helping with the retreat this coming weekend."

Lisa smiled. "I'm really looking forward to it." Her client paid for the treatment, then left the shop, and Lisa went to the kitchen to put the kettle on.

"Can we choose a crystal?"

Greg looked over to where the boys were looking in the treasure chest in the corner, and he nodded. "One each. And get one for your sister as well." He started to look at the crystals on the table in the centre of the shop.

"What was it you were looking for?"

"Malachite."

Ruby went over to another table and picked up a basket. "These are all the pieces I have in at the moment, are they any good?"

Greg took the basket and looked through the pieces. He picked out one which had an interesting shape and took it to the counter, where the boys were waiting patiently with the three crystals they had picked out. Lisa came out of the kitchen with two mugs of tea.

"Did you guys want drinks?" she asked.

Greg shook his head. "No, we need to get the shopping home, thanks."

Ruby wrapped the crystals up individually, writing their names on the outside wrapping, then she rang them through the till.

Greg paid for them, and put his piece in his pocket.

"We should catch up properly soon," Ruby said. "Why don't you come over for dinner sometime? I wanted to hear more about the manifesting circle."

Greg smiled. "Sure, that sounds good. Maybe after this retreat is over."

Ruby nodded. "Excellent. Have a great weekend, I'm sure it will go really well."

"Thanks. Come on, boys, let's get back."

He waved goodbye to Ruby and Lisa and herded the boys out of the door, making room for the three customers about to enter.

They went across the bridge to where the van was parked.

"Uncle Greg?" Jerry said.

"Yeah?"

"Are you and Mummy going to be together, now that Auntie Violet has gone away?"

Greg's eyes widened and he looked down at the young boy, surprised. "Um, no, Auntie Violet has just gone away for a little while, she will be back," he said, with more confidence than he felt. "Besides, your mum and I are just friends."

Jerry frowned. "Okay. I wouldn't mind having you as a dad."

Greg smiled. "Thank you. I'll still always be your uncle. How about the three of us go and see that new action movie that just came out today? Have a guy's night out?"

His suggestion was met with enthusiastic agreement and

Greg laughed. "Great." He hadn't really thought about the fact that Julie's kids no longer had a father figure in their lives. He knew they had only been to visit their dad a few times in the last couple of years, because he'd taken on a new job that took him overseas a lot. He was sure Julie would agree to their outing, it would give her a break for the evening, and an action movie was exactly the kind of escapism he needed for a few hours too.

Chapter Ten

Violet listened in awe to the beautiful child who was stood on the stage in front of thousands of people, speaking of Angels. She told everyone about her own healing miracle. How she came back from the brink of death on Christmas Day, and how her brother had seen an Angel in her room at the moment of the miracle. Since then, she had been performing her own healing miracles, bringing others back from the brink.

Violet looked around her and saw that the audience were as spellbound as she was by the young girl. She wondered if she would get the chance to speak with her. Her own talk was not until later in the afternoon, so she wondered if she could arrange to meet her. Violet felt very much drawn to the child, and wondered if she was a Child of the Golden Age.

For a few moments after the child finished her talk, there was a hushed silence. Violet began to clap and like a wave rolling through the ocean, everyone began to applaud, and the majority of people got to their feet, giving her a standing ovation.

The child accepted the applause with a maturity and grace far beyond her youth, and Violet was impressed. There was a break in the schedule then, so Violet excused herself to Vivi and Saphron, and headed to the side door of the stage.

She showed her pass to the guy at the door, and then went backstage. There was a flurry of activity there, and Violet weaved in and out of people rushing around to where the child was sitting in a chair in the corner, talking to another speaker. Violet waited at a respectful distance until their conversation concluded, then she approached the young girl.

"Velvet!" Kasey said.

Violet stopped suddenly, shocked. "What? How do you know that?"

Kasey smiled and patted the seat next to her. Violet sat down.

"I spoke to an Angel in my dreams last night, and he told me all about you, and said that our paths would cross today. You look a little bit different though." She reached up to touch Violet's hair. "You had white hair in my dream."

Violet's eyes widened. "Who was the Angel you spoke to?"

Kasey tilted her head to one side. "I think his name was Tektite. Which is an odd name. He told me that we needed to connect, because together we could Awaken more people."

Violet didn't know what to say. She believed in synchronicity, but in that moment, it all seemed too strange to be true.

"I'm looking forward to your talk later about the Earth Angel Training Academy, I feel quite strongly that we once met there, long ago. When I went there with my siblings from the Crystal World."

"You are a Crystal Child?" Violet asked, feeling awed.

"Yes, and I remember two Faeries teaching us what it is like to be on Earth. But when I arrived, the energies were so harsh, I forgot how to protect myself, and I became very ill."

"You didn't mention that part in your talk," Violet said with a smile.

Kasey laughed. "My talk is already far too unbelievable by most people's beliefs. To add in my memories of my previous incarnation as a Crystal would just be one step too far, I believe. I don't wish to alienate people, I wish to Awaken and enlighten them."

Violet nodded. She was feeling oddly emotional, speaking to such a pure, beautiful soul.

"I believe we are meant to work together, Velvet. After this conference, and your travels, we must meet up and make a plan. It's important."

"I would very much like that." Violet glanced at her watch. "I must go, my friends are waiting and I need to prepare for my talk. I'm so glad I followed my intuition to come and find you."

Kasey smiled. "I am too." She reached across to hug Violet, and the Old Soul responded by wrapping her arms around the slim child. She breathed in deeply and felt a deep feeling of calm and love wash over her. Her lingering grief over saying goodbye to Laguz receded and her head felt clearer. She pulled back and smile down at the Child.

"Thank you."

Kasey smiled back. "You're welcome, Velvet."

Violet left Kasey backstage and went out to the main hall to find Vivi and Saphron waiting for her.

"Did you get to speak with her?" Saphron asked. "She was amazing."

Violet nodded. "She knew who I was, she dreamed of me last night. Then she hugged me, and I swear she healed a broken part of me with that hug."

"Wow," Vivi said. "That's amazing! I hope we get to meet her too."

"She feels we need to work together, so I think we will be talking later today, I can introduce you to her then."

"That would be great," Saphron said. "Are you ready for your talk?"

Violet nodded. "Yes, I am. I was feeling a bit nervous about it before, but I'm actually quite excited about it now!"

Vivi grinned. "You'll be awesome. Come on, let's go and get a drink before the next speaker."

Violet nodded and followed her friends out of the hall to the bar, her mind still trying to process what had just happened with the Crystal Child.

* * *

Pearl knew that her mouth was wide open in shock, but she

couldn't bring herself to close it.

"I know. It's not what you expected me to say, quite honestly, I never expected to say it either, but after several more messages from Starlight," Gold held up the vial which held only a single pink drop. "I have decided that I cannot resist any longer. I am going to Earth."

"Gold," Pearl said, finally finding her voice. "I am so pleased for you! I'm just in shock, I never thought you would go. Are you becoming a walk in? Or just appearing?"

"I will be appearing there, as myself. My younger self, admittedly," Gold said, a smile on his face. "I know that age gaps in relationships aren't a big issue these days, but I don't think Starlight would wish to be with someone who looks like her grandfather."

Pearl chuckled. "True. Wow, I'm still taking it in. Is the Indigo Child ready to take your place?"

Gold nodded. "Yes, she has been with me for long enough, she has seen most of the different possible crossings, and she knows she can call on the other Elders, or you, if in need of extra assistance."

"Of course she can. Do you have a plan for when you get there? Does Starlight know you are coming?"

Gold shook his head. "Starlight does not know of my arrival. I plan to arrive on the same hillside that you and your team arrived on, so I will be within walking distance of Starlight's home. But I won't go to her immediately, I know of an Elder in the area who will give me a place to stay and help get me set up with the human necessities. Then I will see about meeting Starlight. I know she is still with her husband, I don't wish to go barging in there, and mess up her life."

Pearl smiled. "I'm sure she won't think you are messing up her life. I'm sure she will be thrilled that you found the courage to follow this new and uncertain path to be with her on Earth."

Gold smiled. "Thank you, Angel. I will miss your counsel." He stepped forward to embrace her, and Pearl accepted his hug readily. She stepped back and saw the rune necklace around his neck. She reached up to touch it.

"I had no idea when Starlight told me that she would not

be coming home, that this is what would end up happening." She smiled up at her oldest friend. "I guess it's true, what you always say. Anything really is possible."

"Indeed. I must go now, I have a meeting with the Elders, and then I will be making my transition."

"So soon? Wow, I wish you the very best of luck, please send my love to Starlight, and to her family."

Gold nodded. "I will. Goodbye, Pearl."

"Peace, love and light be with you always," she replied.

"And with you."

Pearl watched Gold disappear into the mists and sighed. She hadn't had any updates from Aragonite on the timeline, and she wondered if she should have warned Gold about the possibility that he would only have a few years there before the world took an irreversible downturn.

She shook her head to herself. Aragonite was going to fix it, she was certain. Telling Gold would just cause more negativity and suffering. Besides, perhaps his return to Earth would shift the world back onto the positive timeline, he was a powerful force, after all.

She sighed again. Things seemed so incredibly complicated since the Angels had begun to meddle in the fate of the world. She wished she could just go back to her simple existence, standing at the gates of the Angelic Realm, welcoming souls home again.

* * *

Greg stared into the flames of the campfire, mesmerised by the dancing orange and yellow fire. Despite Amy having to leave early because her mother had been taken ill, the first retreat without Violet had gone well, and Greg had been too busy with preparing food, doing healing sessions and workshops, and running around keeping everyone happy, to think too much about his wife.

But now that everyone had gone home, and only he and Julie and Lisa remained, his thoughts returned.

"Penny for them," Lisa said, settling next to him on the log, holding her hands out toward the flames to warm up.

Greg smiled at her. "I was just thinking about how well this weekend went. You guys were amazing; it all ran like clockwork. I can't thank you all enough."

Lisa nodded. "It did all go remarkably well. I think all of the participants got a lot out of it. Did you see the change in Bill's posture after than healing session you did with him? It was remarkable, you could visibly see the weight of his past lifted from his shoulders."

"It was incredible," Greg agreed. "I love it when the results are as tangible as that, even though I know that often, the results of a healing don't become apparent until much later after a session."

"Yes, often it's more subtle. I experience that with my clients too."

They sat in silence for a few moments, both watching the flames and appreciating the warmth in the cool evening air.

"Greg."

"Lisa."

They looked at each other and laughed. Lisa motioned for him to speak first.

Greg sighed. "I just wanted to apologise for the other week. I didn't mean to cross any boundaries, I was in a weird place after Violet left, and after that vision of us both as Merpeople, I felt close to you. But I didn't mean to make you feel uncomfortable. I'm sorry."

Lisa smiled and patted his knee. "It's okay, I mean, it did feel a little odd, and I could sense your energy and that you were attracted to me in that moment. But I know how you felt, how you feel. Even though Joseph and I never actually got to have a relationship, I feel the loss of him acutely every day, and I must admit, I miss the physical contact, I miss the companionship. Sometimes, you just really need a hug, you know?"

Greg nodded, his eyes prickling. He shifted closer and wrapped his arm around her. She rested her head against him and he rested his cheek on her head.

They sat like that until Julie came out with mugs of hot chocolate.

"Kids are asleep! Oh, sorry," she stopped suddenly at the sight of them embracing and Lisa sat up straight, and Greg slowly took his arm from around her.

He stood up to take two mugs from her. "Sit down and join us, we should make a toast to how well the retreat went."

Julie frowned, but took a seat next to Lisa. The three of them held their mugs up to clink them together.

"To a very successful retreat, may there be many more to come!"

Lisa and Julie murmured their agreements, but all Greg could feel was Julie's gaze on him. He sighed, it seemed he would have some explaining to do in the morning.

Chapter Eleven

The Angelic Intervention Team were all buzzing with the news of Gold returning to Earth. Emerald found Mica sitting in meditation in the resting room. She sat opposite and waiting impatiently for him to open his eyes.

"What is it?" he asked.

"Gold has decided. He is going to Earth. Aragonite is going to do a showing of the bigger picture to see how much this new development will change the timeline. He thinks it is what's needed to shift back onto the more positive timeline."

Mica's eyes widened. "I honestly didn't think he'd do it. I was sure he was against ever returning after what happened last time."

Emerald sighed. "I know, no one should have to endure that. But I hope that this time will be different. I feel that him reuniting with Starlight will have a huge energetic impact on the Flames. I feel it will create a ripple effect, and that unconditional love will overcome the hate that currently resides. I think it will bring all Flames together."

"That would be amazing. When do we get to review the bigger picture?"

"Very soon. Aragonite is rounding up the teams. Shall we go and get seats?"

Mica nodded and rose to his feet and Emerald did the same.

They left the quiet room, and both noticed the buzz all around. The Angels were all very excited about the new development.

They went to the viewing room, and found that most of the Angels were already there, chattering away.

After a few minutes, Aragonite went to the front of the room. He cleared his throat and the chatter died down.

"I know you have all heard about Gold deciding to return to Earth, and are excited to know how this will affect the timeline. I, too, am eager to know if it has shifted the world back to the positive timeline, and while I am happy to show you the bigger picture as it will be with this new development, I'm afraid I have some bad news." He held up the bottle. "There is only one drop left. Once we view the bigger picture today, unless we can get more of this liquid from Starlight, we will no longer be able to see what effect we are having. So I would like to put it to a vote. Put your hand up if you would like to see the bigger picture today. Or, if you would prefer to keep this until a later date when Gold has settled on Earth, and we have made more changes, leave your hand down. It will go to a majority vote."

"What do you think is for the best?" Olivine asked the Angel.

Aragonite sighed. "It would be good to see it today, so we can adjust our strategies accordingly, based on the changes this will create. But part of me would prefer to keep it, so that we can check at a later date. I fear that if this hasn't created the shift we need, it will lower our energies. But ultimately, it is not my decision, it is all of ours. We work as a team here. So, all in favour of watching today, please raise your hands."

A scattering of hands went up, less than a quarter, Emerald guessed. Though she was so incredibly curious to see the possible changes, she'd kept her hand down. She felt it would be better to keep it for a later date, though she did wonder if she could get more liquid from Starlight.

"Okay, I'm afraid there will be no showing of the bigger picture today. We will keep this last drop for when we feel we cannot continue our work without knowing what direction the world is going in. I'm sorry you have all gathered here for no reason, please feel free to return to your activities."

The Angels began to disperse, the mood a little more sombre than before.

"Would you like to for a walk?" Mica asked as they stood. "It feels as though we have been here for an age, I would like to get some fresh air and exercise."

Emerald smiled. "You're still really quite human sometimes, Mike." She winked at him as she used his human name.

Mica smiled. "I do miss the woods around the Retreat. There was something quite magical about them. Especially when the leaves changed colour in the autumn. As much as raking them up was a huge pain, it was such a beautiful sight."

Emerald nodded. "I miss being there too. I miss many human treats, such as baking my famous chocolate cake, and building a good fire in the wood burner in the winter, and snuggling under the covers together, while it snowed outside."

They walked to the entrance, and stepped outside into the light. "Do you think we will ever have another human life?" Mica asked.

Emerald linked her arm in his and shook her head. "I spoke with Pallas about this when I returned. I'm pretty certain we won't. I think we are needed here too much. Especially if Aragonite chooses to go to Earth to find Cotton."

"What? Aragonite is leaving?"

Emerald looked around to make sure no one was nearby, and she hushed him. "Shh, I wasn't meant to tell anyone. Aragonite asked me if I thought it was a good idea for him to become human. His Flame, Blue Cotton, believes that she will not be reunited with him in this lifetime, and she is currently fulfilling her mission. So I told him that if he did decide to go, it shouldn't be just yet. Otherwise the intensity of the reunion may derail her from her path."

"Wise advice," Mica commented. "How incredible though. Two Twin Flame reunions which seemed utterly improbable are now happening. Surely that will have a huge effect on the new timeline, especially as they didn't happen at all in the old one."

"I would have thought so." Emerald realised they were meandering toward the lake. "Is there something you wanted to see?"

Mica shook his head. "Not really, we have been watching Earth so much, I feel like I have been there more than I have been here, I just thought it would be nice to sit by the water."

Emerald smiled. "It is nice to get some fresh air." She looked around the lake and frowned. "There doesn't seem to be many Angels working. Where do you think they all are?"

"Probably where we have been. You have to admit: it is far more interesting working with Aragonite than here at the lake. It is frustrating, whispering advice that falls on deaf ears. It is far more satisfying to nudge someone and see them actually make the change."

"I do worry though," Emerald said as they settled on the pebbly shore. "That it is too easy to feel like a God, moving the humans and Earth Angels like pawns in a game of chess. Ultimately, we are playing a very risky game, nudging them in the way we are, to fulfil our strategies. What if we can't change the timeline to the better outcome? What if it does end up in darkness and chaos, and it's all because of us?"

Mica sighed. "We just have to remain positive that it will improve again. And besides, technically, the world has already come to an end. This is really a second chance, and if we want to try and make the Golden Age a reality, we must do what we have never dared to do before. Which means not being afraid to make mistakes, or go off course once in a while."

Emerald sighed. "I know you are right."

"I usually am," Mica replied with a grin. "Now, can we just enjoy the water and the peace for a while? Trust that it will all work out well. We have the best in the Realm working on it."

"Okay." Emerald leaned into his side, and he wrapped his arm around her, and their wings wrapped around them both.

*　*　*

"Your visit has gone by too fast!"

Violet hugged her new friends tightly. "It really has," she agreed, tears in her eyes. "Let's meet again soon, and keep in touch as much as we can."

"Of course," Saphron said, wiping her eyes. "Now that we

have found each other again, we cannot lose each other. I want to interview you for my radio show again soon too."

Violet smiled. "Yeah, that was fun the other night! I really enjoyed it. I thought I would be nervous, but I think that Kasey removed all my nerves surrounding doing things like that."

"Meeting her was amazing, I think you two will do some incredible work together," Vivi said. "And my back pain has completely disappeared since she hugged me. I've had that pain for years."

Violet's tram arrived, and she picked up her suitcase. "Thank you, both of you, for your love and friendship, I'm so pleased we had this time together."

Both women nodded, tears in their eyes. "Have a safe journey," Saphron said.

Violet nodded and stepped onto the tram, putting her fare into the box by the driver.

She walked up the aisle and sat down, then waved to her friends as the tram surged forward. She wiped her tears with her sleeve. It felt like she was losing them all over again, as she had at the Academy, when each of the professors had been called to Earth. During a reading she had done for Vivi, it seemed that she had been a second year trainee at the Academy. She was from the Angelic Realm, and in the reading, Violet had been able to tell Vivi her name, and also the name of her Flame. She smiled to herself at the memory. She hoped that Vivi would find her Flame. She was such a beautiful Angel, she absolutely deserved to experience a wonderful union.

Her thoughts of Twin Flames of course made her think of Greg, and she sighed. By the end of her visit, she still hadn't been able to admit to her two new friends that they were currently separated. She twisted her wedding ring on her finger, which was a simple, silver band. She slipped it off, and traced the word engraved inside with her finger.

Eternity.

Since her meeting with Kasey, the Crystal Child who seemed to be truly creating miracles, the pain of their separation had lessened, and she felt able to live with whatever the outcome turned out to be.

She slipped the ring back on her finger.

One thing she knew for certain was that whether they reunited in this lifetime or not, she would always love him deeply. For eternity.

* * *

"Gold! Welcome, my dear old friend!"

Gold nodded and stepped into the home of the Elder he had contacted before leaving the Other Side. He was ushered into the living room, where a cheerful fire was blazing in the hearth. He went over to it to absorb some heat, feeling chilled to the bone after walking down the hill. Being in a human body, a young, slim one at that, was colder than Gold had remembered. But then his previous incarnation had been somewhere much warmer than the UK.

"Would you like a hot drink to warm up?" Jaron asked him.

Gold nodded. "Yes please. Do you have any hot chocolate? A young Faerie I know always went on about it, and I have been curious."

Jaron chuckled. "Yes, I can rustle up a hot chocolate, please, make yourself at home."

Gold thanked his friend, then sat in a cosy armchair. He looked around the room, and spied a photograph of Jaron and a woman. He frowned. She looked familiar.

A few minutes later, Jaron reappeared with a mug and put it on the small coffee table next to Gold's chair. "Be careful, it's quite hot."

"Who is the lady, Jaron?" he asked, pointing to the photograph.

Jaron smiled. "That's my wife. She went home earlier this year."

Gold nodded. "Yes, I remember her. She was worried about leaving you, she didn't want you to have to cook for yourself, she said you always burnt things."

Jaron laughed. "That's my Lana! She always took care of me, and always did the cooking. Said I couldn't be trusted in the kitchen." He picked the photograph up and stroked it. "But we both knew it was time. She was ready."

Gold picked up the hot chocolate and took a small sip. It was as heavenly as Aria had described. "Yes, she was. She returned to the Angelic Realm, and I think she is doing great work there."

"Thank you, Gold," Jaron said. Setting the frame back on the mantelpiece. "That makes me so much happier, knowing she is okay."

He went back to the kitchen, then returned and settled in the other armchair with his own mug of hot chocolate.

"So what's the plan? What do I need to get sorted for you? Money isn't an issue, so I can set you up with the clothing and any essentials you need. And there is a room here for as long as you need it or want it."

"Thank you, all of that is needed and much appreciated. Once I have acclimatised, I guess I will seek out contact with Starlight." He sighed. "I only hope that she really did want me to come here, and that disrupting her home life will be worth it."

"I'm sure it will all work out well." Jaron stared at Gold for a few moments. "It's so odd seeing you in your youth again. You really are quite a handsome guy."

Gold chuckled and Jaron joined in. Soon the two old friends were laughing raucously while the fire crackled and popped in the background.

Chapter Twelve

Violet looked around the roomful of Earth Angels who had come to hear her speak, and smiled. She tried to look each of them in the eye, and deeply appreciate all of them for taking the time to come and meet her. She was in New York City, and was loving every moment. Though she had of course been to London, and cities across Europe, this was her first time in America, and though it all felt very big and unfamiliar, she had a weird feeling that she was finally home. She knew that throughout her many previous lives she'd lived in America, but she remembered few details of them now.

When everyone quieted down, and the attention of the room was on her, Violet stood up and welcomed them.

"Beautiful Earth Angels, thank you so much for coming here tonight, for taking the time out of your busy schedules to come and learn more about Earth Angels, and what it means to be one." She picked up a copy of her book. "When I began my spiritual awakening, I had no idea that I would be writing a book, and that the book would speak to so many. Though it is a work of fiction, much of the events and characters are based on real people and situations, and since writing it, I have met so many more of the characters within it. It's a story of how the Angels, Faeries, Merpeople and Starpeople have come to Earth to help people Awaken. First, they attend an Academy on the

Other Side, to learn how to be human. Because, let's face it, it ain't easy."

The audience laughed and Violet smiled. It felt so natural to be in front of a group of people, it reminded her of being at the Academy. She needed to thank Kasey for taking away her nervousness and her doubt in herself. As she continued talking about the Earth Angels, she knew that she believed in what she was sharing, and that it would help the people in the room a great deal.

She talked for half an hour, then invited them to ask questions, which she answered as best as she could. Unsurprisingly, most of the questions were about Twin Flames, which she at least felt well prepared to answer. It seemed that as in the UK, Flames in America were reuniting, but then separating again. Many were struggling with the separation. She gave them a summarised version of the advice she would give in her retreats, and hoped it would help. At the end of the session, Violet signed a dozen books, and received many hugs.

The last person in line stood out to Violet. During the evening, she had asked a question about the purpose of the Angels, and just from her appearance, Violet could see she was originally from the Angelic Realm. Violet smiled up at her now, and saw the sadness in the woman's eyes.

"Did you want me to sign a book?" she asked.

The woman shook her head. "No, I can't afford it right now. I just wanted to say thank you. You've helped me to make a decision I've been trying to make for a while."

Violet smiled at the woman, but had an uneasy feeling in the pit of her stomach. "You're welcome, I'm glad it was useful to you."

The woman nodded then walked away, and Violet frowned. She wondered what the decision had been. She could almost literally see a dark cloud over her head.

"Hey, how did it go?"

Violet looked up to see Mandy, an Earth Angel she'd once met in London at a seminar, who'd offered to host her while she was in the city.

"It was amazing," Violet said. "I really enjoyed it." She

looked at the doorway but the woman had already left. She wondered if she should have pursued a conversation with her.

Mandy smiled. "That's great. Sorry I missed it. Work ran late, so I got a taxi, then there was a jam on 5th Avenue."

Violet shook her head. "No worries, shall we go?" She picked up her bag and said goodbye to the staff at the busy holistic bookstore, and the two women stepped out into the city.

"How was work?" Violet asked as they headed toward to subway.

"It was busy. We're already working on the fall line, and I'm in charge of designing the new range of sweaters. It's fun, but really tiring."

Violet smiled. "I bet. I'm so pleased that you got the job you wanted. And living in the Big Apple now too! That's really brilliant."

"It happened because I used the manifestation technique you taught at your seminar in London! I had been really struggling to get any work at all before that."

"I should get you to write a testimonial for my website," Violet said with a laugh.

"Of course. Just tell me how long it needs to be and where to send it."

The two women descended into the nearest subway station, and were just in time to step onto the next train. They sat down, and when Violet glanced around, her eyes met those of the woman from the bookshop. Violet smiled at her, but the woman just looked away.

Suddenly, a loud ringing noise started up in Violet's left ear, a sign that Violet had always taken to be the Angels trying to get her attention.

Violet turned to Mandy. "Can I meet you back at the apartment?" she asked quietly.

Mandy frowned but nodded. "Sure, you have a key. You okay to get back alone?"

Violet nodded. She looked over and saw that the woman was stood up, waiting to get off at the next stop. Violet smiled at Mandy, then got up and followed the woman off the train. She had absolutely no idea why she was doing it, but the ringing in her ear was getting louder and she had a twisting feeling in her gut that she couldn't ignore. Despite feeling exhausted from a busy day and the talk that evening, she found that a renewed energy ran through her, and she picked up her pace to keep the woman in her sights as they went through the station, up the stairs, and emerged into the bustling city.

Sirens blared somewhere in the distance, people in bars were laughing, the traffic was whizzing by. It was an assault on the senses compared to the blissful calm of the woods around the Twin Flame Retreat, and though it was new and exciting, Violet felt a twinge of longing for the peace and quiet of home.

She followed the Angel down the street, and tried to figure out exactly what her plan was going to be. Would she confront her? Talk to her? Just follow her to make sure she was safe?

As Violet mused, she realised that the woman had stopped suddenly, and was about to step out into the street, right in front of the oncoming traffic.

"No!" Violet gasped. She ran toward the woman, grabbed a handful of her jacket and yanked her backwards, just as a taxi whizzed by, horn blaring.

Violet lost her balance and the two women toppled backwards, hitting the concrete hard. Gasping, Violet tried to catch her breath, the wind knocked out of her.

"What are you doing?" the woman cried. She looked at Violet. "You? Did you follow me?"

Still gasping, Violet nodded. "I could tell there was something wrong, I felt I had to."

The woman began to cry, and Violet noticed vaguely that the crowds of people were just walking around them, completely oblivious to what had just transpired. When Violet finally managed to catch her breath and slow her heart rate down a little, she shifted into a sitting position, feeling sore from the fall. She got to her feet, and held a hand out to the woman.

The woman looked at her hand, tears streaming down her cheeks. After a moment, she took it, and Violet pulled her to her feet. She picked up her bag, and handed it to her.

"What's your name, Angel?"

"Verity," the woman replied.

Violet pulled a tissue from her bag and handed it to Verity. "Let's go get a drink, and have a chat, Verity. The Angels have brought us together for a reason."

Verity blew her nose and nodded. "Okay."

They walked for a block before they found a coffee shop that was still open, and they went inside. After ordering and collecting the drink and cakes, Violet joined Verity on the sofa in the corner.

"Well? Are you going to tell me what's going on?"

Verity sighed. "It's hard to know where to begin. You're right, it's no accident that I ended up at your talk this evening. I was looking for answers, for confirmation of my thoughts, and I got exactly that tonight."

Violet frowned. "I don't understand, what confirmation did you get?"

"That going home was the best option for me. To return to the Angelic Realm." She looked at Violet, tears running down her cheeks again. "I can't stay here anymore, Violet. It's too harsh. I've lost everything and everyone I care about, and I was hanging on by my fingernails, and then I saw the poster for your talk. So I came along, and hearing you talk about the Other Side, about the Angelic Realm, made me realise that I could just go home. I could leave this awful place, leave behind the pain, the hate, the suffering, and be whole and happy again."

Violet sat back, feeling shocked. She had assumed that if the Earth Angels knew where they'd come from, it would be easier for them to stay on Earth, not that it would make them desperate to return home.

"So you decided to walk into the traffic so you could go home?"

"It seemed like the easiest option."

Tears formed in Violet's eyes and she looked at the lost, broken Angel before her, and her heart thudded. "Oh, Angel, I'm so sorry that you felt that your only option was to go home. My intention wasn't to make Earth Angels want to leave!"

"I know, but you have no idea how hard it's been, how much it hurts to be here. I gave up my friends and family, moved to the other side of the country to be with my Flame, then he decided that he didn't want me after all, and left." She sighed. "I cannot go back to my family, they won't understand. They thought I was crazy to follow him here, and I told them they just didn't understand how much we loved each other." Her voice broke, and her shoulders began to shake.

Violet reached out and put her hand on the Angel's arm. "Oh, my sweet Angel. I'm so sorry. But yes, I do know how hard it is to lose a Flame." Her mind flashed back to the moment Greg pushed her away, to the moment she walked into the sea, determined to go home herself.

"I know exactly how much that hurts, and I also know that it seems like the easiest thing, the best thing, to go home and leave all of this pain behind." She sighed. "But it's not. I know it seems like a lot to ask, but I truly believe that you have more to do here. That your purpose isn't finished. That it's possible for you to find happiness again, here on Earth."

Verity frowned. "How do you know that?"

"Because my Flame left me too. And it was the end of my world. I didn't want to exist on this planet without him, but, ultimately, going home wasn't the answer. Because I had family, and friends who loved me, who would have missed me so much. And because it is possible find happiness and fulfil your purpose on Earth without your Flame. You are enough as you are." Violet left out the part where she went home and returned from the Other Side. It was too complicated to explain.

Verity didn't look convinced. "What am I supposed to do then? I have no reason to keep going. And I cannot afford to stay here in the city, it's just too expensive."

"It's time to go home. Not to the Other Side, but to your family. I think they will understand, and I think they will welcome you home with open arms."

Verity was quiet for a while. "How can you be so sure?"

"Because you're an Angel. And Angels find it so hard to reach out and ask for help, and they spend their lives helping everyone else and not themselves. If you reach out to your family and friends, and allow them to help you, they will be so happy, I promise."

"And you really think I can be happy too?"

Violet smiled and reached out to hug the Angel. "I'm sure of it."

"Thank you."

Violet pulled away, and the two women ate their cakes and finished their drinks. Violet was beginning to feel very weary. She glanced at her phone and saw that it was approaching eleven o'clock. She really needed some sleep.

"It's late," Verity said. "Where do you need to get back to?"

Violet told her Mandy's address, and the Angel gave her directions to find her way back. They left the coffee shop, and Violet reached out to hug the Angel again.

"Thank you, Violet," Verity said in her ear. "I will call my mom in the morning."

Violet pulled a card out of her pocket. She handed it to Verity. "If you get into this dark place again, call me, or email me. I know that you can do this, that you have more love and happiness yet to experience in this lifetime."

Verity took the card and smiled. "I will. Goodnight, Violet."

"Goodnight, Verity."

Violet turned and headed back to the subway, and followed Verity's instructions back to Mandy's apartment.

Mandy was in the kitchen when she let herself in.

"Oh, thank goodness you're back okay, what happened?"

Violet sat at the breakfast counter, and accepted the cup of tea she was offered. Mandy had found some British tea especially for Violet's visit, for which Violet was very grateful. The Americans really didn't do tea in quite the same way.

When Violet explained what had happened with Verity, Mandy's eyes widened.

"Wow, you saved her from killing herself?"

Violet sighed. "Yes. Or at least, from severe injury." She shook her head. "It's made me question what I am doing though. I mean, I thought I was helping Earth Angels to find their purpose, to be unafraid to live, because death just means that we go home. But apparently I'm making death sound far more inviting than living."

"I'm sure that's not the case for everyone, it's just that this lady was on the edge, in need of an escape, and she took your words and fit them to what she wanted."

Violet sighed. "I hope so. Because I really don't want the Earth Angels to go home because of what I've said. That makes me feel really sad."

"I'm just glad you followed your intuition tonight. And in the morning, I'm sure that Verity will be glad too."

Violet yawned. "I hope so. I need some sleep. It's been an eventful day."

Mandy laughed. "It has been that. I'm at work again tomorrow, but you have the spare key. Go and explore. You might as well see as much of the city as you can before you leave for Arizona."

Violet nodded and took her cup to the sink in the kitchen "I was thinking of going up the Rockefeller Centre and taking some pictures."

"Sounds good. Remember to take a sweater though. It's warm at street level, but when you step out onto the roof it can be really cold."

"Good tip, thanks." Violet gave Mandy a hug goodnight, then went to her room. She only just managed to change into her nightclothes and brush her teeth before collapsing into bed and immediately falling asleep.

When she awoke the next morning, Mandy had already left for work, and there were fresh bagels on the counter and a note saying to help herself. Violet did just that, and also made herself a cup of coffee.

She looked at a map of the city, and plotted the major places she wanted to visit. She was looking forward to exploring some of the side streets too, to see what delights were hidden there.

Once she was full, she showered and dressed, then picked up the spare key to the apartment, and headed out the door. She joined the throng of people on the sidewalk, all looking very determined about getting to their destinations. She walked slowly, wanting to take in all the sounds and smells and sights around her.

She was looking at a particularly beautiful shop window

display when she bumped into someone, and nearly sent them flying. "Oh! Sorry!" she gasped.

The person didn't even stop to accept her apology, they just kept marching. She shook her head, and moved out of the way of the flow. She leaned against the building, and a sign across the street that was flickering caught her attention.

'Crystal Ball Readings $5'

She smiled. It had been a while since she'd had a reading, and the idea of having a crystal ball reading in New York City really appealed to her. She found the nearest crossing and went across the street, and entered the tiny store. It was musty and dark inside, and the smell of years of incense being burned filled her nostrils and irritated them.

She rubbed her nose and ventured further into the store, past an interesting collection of herbs, candles and journals.

At the rear of the store, she found a man hunched over a table, staring into a crystal ball. She was a little surprised, having expected to find a woman there.

"Could I have a reading?" she asked, beginning to feel a little bit creeped out.

The man looked up at her slowly, nodded once, then looked back at the ball.

Violet sat down opposite him, and didn't have to wait long before he began to speak.

When he finished the reading and looked up at her and asked for the payment, Violet was in shock. She paid him and hurried out of the store, not stopping to catch her breath until she was a block away.

Surely it was just a scam. There's no way that what he predicted could come to pass, was there?

* * *

A week after the retreat, Greg was in his workshop, tinkering with an idea for an alternative heating system for the house.

"Cuppa?"

He looked up to the doorway where Julie stood and smiled. "Yes, please," he said, holding his hand out to accept the hot drink from her. He took a sip and set it down on the counter. "Kids okay?"

Julie nodded. "Yeah, thank goodness there's so much for them to do around here. It keeps them busy and out of my hair."

"There's plenty of places to explore. As long as they don't go down to the caves."

Julie shook her head. "Don't worry, I think we've definitely quashed that idea out of them. They know not to leave the general vicinity of the house, and to check in with me regularly."

"They're good kids," Greg said. "You've done a great job with them."

Julie smiled. "Thank you. I have wondered, on more than one occasion, if leaving their dad, leaving their home and bringing them on this mad adventure was really the right thing for them, but they appear to be thriving."

"When are they seeing their dad next? The boys are missing him, I think. They were asking me if I was going to be their new dad."

Julie blushed and laughed. "Oh dear! Sorry if that made things awkward. I think they just enjoy your company, and I suppose we spend a lot of time together."

Greg shrugged. "It didn't bother me. I told them that we could do some fun stuff together. They're fun to have around." There were a few moments of silence, and Greg sipped his cooling tea.

"Is there something happening between you and Lisa?"

Greg choked on his sip, and coughed several times. "What?" he croaked.

"You and Lisa seem to be very close since Violet left. I know it's really not any of my business, but Lisa and Violet are both my friends, and, well, yeah," Julie looked down at her feet, shifting uncomfortably.

"No," Greg said firmly. He set his mug down and put his hand on her arm. "There's nothing going on between me and Lisa. She was missing her Twin Flame, I was missing Violet, and we just provided each other with a shoulder to lean on. She's also trying to help me heal my past life issues. That's all."

Julie looked into his eyes and saw the truth within them. She nodded. "I'm sorry. It's really none of my business. And I get it, I mean, I've never even met my Flame in this life, but I still miss him every day. I'm glad you're helping each other."

Greg smiled. "Why don't you have a healing session with Lisa? We both saw a memory of our lives as Merpeople last time. It was quite interesting."

Julie's eyes widened. "Really? That's incredible." She sighed. "I don't know what she could do for me. My Flame is in another Universe. I just need to accept that we're not going to be together this time, and let go of him. Maybe then I could find someone else that I can love, that could be a father figure for the kids."

"Lisa could probably help you with letting go too. She's a very powerful healer."

Julie nodded. "I will ask her. Thanks. Anyway, I'll let you get back to it. I need to update the website and get advertising the next retreat as well as gather the testimonials from the last one."

Greg sighed. "Thank you for taking on that side of the business, I really don't think I could have done it all myself. I was never very good with the technical stuff."

"It really is my pleasure. You and Violet welcomed me and the kids here with no hesitation, and I am so very thankful for that. Besides, it's all part of my mission to help Earth Angels to make a living from their passions." She waved goodbye and went back to the house.

Greg drank the rest of his tea, then went back to his sketch pad.

Chapter Thirteen

Emerald was meeting with the other team leaders again, and she was pleased to hear of the progress being made on Earth. Surely they must be shifting the world onto a more positive timeline?

"Violet's tour is going really well, her talks are well attended and received, and her book sales are increasing. Many Earth Angels have been Awoken thanks to her appearances and the book. The ripples of Awakening are getting bigger and spreading further," Tektite reported. "She also connected with Kasey, as we had hoped. And when they both are in the UK again, they will work together. If Kasey attends the Twin Flame Retreats and heals the Flames there, then the chances of more harmonious reunions are so much higher. We envision Kasey and Violet working together more than once."

Emerald smiled. "I would love to have met Kasey myself. I have watched her on Earth. What a beautiful, pure hearted Crystal Child."

"She is incredible. And I believe it's partly because of her death in the original timeline that the world did not Awaken enough," Olivine said. "The world had no chance without her light."

"I am so very hopeful that we have shifted the world back onto the path toward the Golden Age," Labradorite said. "The combination all of our help, and both Velvet and this amazing

Crystal Child working together, not to mention Gold being there and the Flames finally reuniting in harmony; it gives me a good feeling. I think it's all finally going to work."

"It is going to work."

The Angels looked up to see Aragonite there, a huge grin on his face. "I am certain of it."

"How can you know? We haven't seen the bigger picture in quite a while," Emerald said, curious.

"Because I visited Starlight while she slept, and I asked her to show me. She was unable to give me any more of the liquid, but she showed me through her eyes. And all of the changes we have made have altered things for the better again. We have corrected the course, and the world is fast reaching the tipping point that will pull us easily into the Golden Age."

The Angels all gasped in delight. "So we've done it? We've changed things?" Tektite asked.

"We must continue on our course, we still need to make the nudges and ensure that things run smoothly for those who are at the forefront of the changes, but yes, we have done it."

Unable to contain her excitement, Emerald began to clap, and after a moment, the other Angels joined in. When the noise died down, Olivine asked Aragonite when he would be announcing the good news to the rest of the teams.

"Now. I just wanted to tell you seven first. And to thank you. I know that you could be doing much more pleasurable pursuits than being inside all the time, staring into basins of water, and I appreciate your dedication."

The Angels applauded again, this time for each other. When they quieted down, Aragonite motioned to Emerald to follow him outside.

"What is it?" she asked.

"Now that I am certain that everything is going to go well, I cannot wait any longer. I must return to Earth to my Blue. I spoke to Starlight about it, and she said that she couldn't see any reason why I should delay any further. Do you see any reason to?"

Emerald appreciated that he respected her opinion of the situation, but she also felt uneasy at having to make such a big decision. She still had no idea if it was the right thing to do. What if it pulled Julie off course, and that then irrevocably changed the new timeline for the worse?

Aware that he was awaiting her wisdom, she said the only thing she could in that situation. "Follow your heart, Angel. Then you cannot go wrong."

Aragonite's entire face lit up, and he picked Emerald up and swung her around, taking her completely by surprise and making her squeal.

"Thank you, Emerald," he said, kissing her on both cheeks. "Now, I have one last question. Will you and Mica take over from me here? You have both been on Earth recently, you are both passionate about the work, I really can't think of any other Angels who are better suited and qualified for the job."

Emerald blushed, and her thoughts flitted to Tanzanite; he was not going to be impressed by this news at all. "I would be honoured, Aragonite," she said. "And I am sure that Mica would be also."

"Great. I will make the announcements shortly. Let's spend some time together after, to discuss your new role? Bring Mica along too. Once you are both happy, I will be on my way."

"Sounds good. I will see you later."

Aragonite nodded and left, and she headed in the opposite direction to find her Flame to tell him the news.

*   *   *

The heat that welcomed Violet when she stepped out of the airport and into the Phoenix sunshine was something to behold. She felt that if she stood still for more than a few moments, she would actually melt. She glanced up at a digital display that stated the temperature was 115 degrees Fahrenheit. She had no idea what that was in Celsius, but she knew that it was the hottest temperature she had ever experienced.

She saw a flurry of movement and looked to her left to see a man approaching her. She smiled, recognising him from his photo online.

"Robert!" she said, putting her bag down to receive his hug.

"Thank you so much for picking me up, I really appreciate it."

"Of course! Welcome to Arizona! Let's get into the car and cool down." He grabbed her suitcase and she picked up her carry-on bag and followed his long strides back to where he had pulled up in the loading zone. He put her case in the back of the car, then they both got in, and he turned the air conditioning up high. As they pulled out of the airport, Violet stared out of the window in amazement at the desert landscape and all the different shaped cacti.

"How was the flight?"

Violet smiled at Robert. "Longer than I'd expected, a bit boring. But I did manage to write down a few ideas for a possible second book."

"It was productive then, that's good."

"How is your book going? I'm sorry I haven't had a chance to read it yet."

"It's going well, you know how it is, just a case of constantly marketing and making people aware of it. I want to get started on the next book too, I have so many ideas swimming around in my head."

Violet sighed. "I know what you mean. It just feels like there are too many other more 'important' things that need doing. And that just sitting down and writing is lazy or something."

Robert concentrated for a moment to pull out onto the highway, then raised an eyebrow at Violet. "That sounds like a belief that needs changing, if you ask me. Writing is not lazy. How many people has your book helped to Awaken? To heal? That's real work."

Violet smiled. "You're right. I need to change how I see it. After all, I think it was what I came here to Earth to do. Write books that Awaken people to their true origins."

"So how can it be lazy? Following your life's purpose?"

Violet chuckled. "Okay, okay, it's real work, and I will make it more of a priority from now on."

"Atta girl," Robert said. He pulled off the highway and they drove down a wide suburban street, before turning right onto a narrower one. Robert pulled up in front of a house and turned off the engine.

"Nice home," Violet said. "How long have you and your family lived here?"

"About ten years. We like it, it's warm all year round. Can't get too much sunshine, I don't feel."

They got out of the car and Robert carried her suitcase into the house. He gave her a brief tour, then they got cold drinks and went out to the back yard where Violet saw they had a swimming pool. She smiled, glad she had brought a swimsuit with her. It had been a long time since she had gone swimming.

They sat with their feet dangling in the pool, and chatted about their books and marketing ideas until the sun set. Violet found herself yawning profusely. Though she had only flown from New York, it had been a long day, and she felt the need to rest.

She had a snack first, then went to the spare room, and pulled a few essentials from her bag. She got changed and slid under the covers. She had a busy week ahead, with four events happening in different bookstores and venues in Arizona. She would need to be on top form.

Before going to sleep, she checked her phone to see if there were any important messages or emails, as she had done every night of the tour so far. As usual, she was disappointed to find there wasn't a single message from Greg or from her friends. She knew she'd told them to only contact her in an emergency, so no contact was a good thing, but she still felt quite lonely. Even though she was enjoying connecting with new Earth Angels and she felt quite at home in America, she missed her friends, and her home in the woods.

Feeling too awake to sleep now, she remembered that she had a copy of Robert's book on her Kindle, so she got it out of her bag and decided to read a couple of chapters.

An hour later, though desperate to continue reading, her eyes were closing. As she drifted off to sleep, she whispered to the Angels to remove her melancholy, and allow her to fully enjoy the trip.

*   *   *

"Violet is still having trouble letting go," Emerald remarked to Mica. "Even though Kasey healed the broken parts of her, and helped her to release her doubts and fears around her purpose, she still has a dark space inside of her that refuses to lighten, even though the tour is going so well, and everything is going according to plan."

Mica frowned. "Perhaps we should nudge Greg and Lisa together. Maybe if Violet knew that he had moved on, she would let go and move on also."

Emerald looked down at Violet's sleeping face in her basin and frowned. "Really? You think that would be the best thing? To just match him up with a random person so he's no longer available to her?"

"Lisa isn't a random person, she was the closest person that Greg, or rather Laguz, had during his entire existence as a Merman. They were best friends, they pretty much ran the underwater world together. They make a great team, and I certainly saw some chemistry there."

Emerald sighed. "It really doesn't feel good, doing that. I think it would just break Violet's heart, and render her incapable of pursing her missions. We want her to let go of the sadness and really thrive in the present moment. Not fall deeper into the black hole."

"That's easy then. Have her meet someone else."

Emerald's eyes widened. "While on the tour?"

"Sure, why not? She's meeting so many people, why couldn't there be someone in one of her events who asks her out, who she is attracted to? I'm certain we could find an Earth Angel who fits the bill."

Emerald thought about it for a while. She knew that it would upset Greg if Violet met someone else, but he was less likely to be derailed from finding his purpose, and from running the retreats. She sighed. "Let's see if we can find the right person. Perhaps you're right, even if nothing comes of it, maybe it will allow her to let go in order for a reunion to be possible."

Mica nodded and returned to his basin. "I will see if I can spot any possibilities among those thinking of attending her events."

"Emerald!"

The two Angels looked up to see Aragonite approaching. "It is time. I am leaving. Are you both ready?"

Emerald nodded and smiled. "Yes, we are ready, and if we get really stuck, we will visit Starlight or ask Pearl. Go, find Blue. You deserve to be happy together."

Aragonite smiled. "Thank you, both of you." He hugged them both hard. "I have no doubt that if you had not come to find me and hadn't joined the team, then things on Earth wouldn't have shifted enough to make this possible. I am so thankful to you both."

Emerald felt her eyes filling with tears. "You're so welcome, Angel. Please send our regards to everyone at the Twin Flame Retreat, and tell them we are both so proud of them all for keeping it going."

"I will. Peace, love and light be with you always."

"And with you," Emerald and Mica replied simultaneously. They watched the Angel leave, a new spring in his step.

Emerald sighed. It seemed so wrong that Aragonite and Cotton were reuniting, and Gold and Starlight were reuniting, yet there were doing their best to separate Greg and Violet even further. Surely there had to be another way?

"I know what you're thinking, but I still think this is the best course of action," Mica said softly.

Sometimes Emerald hated it when Mica read her thoughts.

And she hated it even more when she knew he was right.

Chapter Fourteen

"Greg?! Are you in?"

Greg frowned at the urgency in Lisa's voice, and yelled out from the kitchen. "Yeah, I'm here!"

He looked up as she ran into the room, her cheeks flushed, a piece of paper clutched in her hand. "It's real! It's actually a real thing!"

Greg shook his head, not understanding what she was talking about. He took the paper she thrust at him, and scanned it. It was an article she'd printed from the internet, about a man in America who had invented a machine to record dreams.

Greg's eyes widened. "The dream recorder? It exists?"

"Yes, and check out the date he had the breakthrough in his invention!"

Greg read the date silently, then frowned and turned to the kitchen calendar. He searched for the date on the calendar, and there, written neatly in Violet's script, were the words 'Manifestation Meeting'.

Greg looked at Lisa. "You think we did this? That he was able to make the breakthrough because of our visualisation and using the Atlantis technique?"

"You have to admit, it's a pretty huge coincidence! What if it just materialised in this guy's lab instead of on the tray in front of us? I think we need to give it another go."

Greg put the paper down and put the kettle on, his mind whirring. "What do you think we should try and create this time?" He thought of his own tinkering. "I'm trying to figure out a new heating system, maybe we could focus on that? There's a couple of points that I'm not sure about how to create."

"That would be cool," Lisa said, sitting down at the counter and accepting the steaming mug and the tin of biscuits. "I thinking that perhaps we could each choose something that we wanted to create, and then focus on that. Now we have proof, we don't have to try and create something that doesn't yet exist, we could just focus on things we know are possible, but that we aren't yet experiencing."

Greg joined her at the counter with his own drink, and a biscuit. "So we'd take it in turns to all focus on each person's wish?"

"Yes, I think the collective energy of the group focussed on each thing will be more powerful."

Greg nodded. "I don't see why not. I mean, like last time, we have nothing to lose." He picked up the paper again, scanning the article. "Are they going to mass produce the invention? So that people can buy it? Or is it just going to be too expensive to make for regular people?"

"I'm not sure, it doesn't say in the article. Still pretty amazing though."

"What's pretty amazing?"

Lisa and Greg looked up to see Julie. Lisa held out the article to her, explained the synchronicity of the date, and their idea to focus on things they would like to manifest.

Julie's eyes grew wider and wider. "Wow. It worked. That's amazing!" She made herself a cup of tea and joined them. "So what do you two want to manifest?"

"I want help with a heating invention I'm working on," Greg said.

"What I want to manifest is not a thing, but more of an experience," Lisa said. "Do you think it will work?"

"What is it?" Julie asked.

"A relationship. A harmonious, happy relationship with a man I can be completely authentic and honest with about who

I really am."

Greg shrugged. "I don't see why that would be a problem. Let's give it a try." He sipped his tea then looked at Julie. "How about you?"

Julie blushed a little. "I would ask for the same as Lisa. I think I'm ready to be with someone. I've let go of my Flame, the kids are settled, I feel like I'm on my mission and won't let anything derail me from that. So I would like to meet someone too."

Greg smiled. "You guy are making me feel bad now, maybe I should be asking for things to work out for me and Violet, instead of help with my heating invention."

Lisa laughed. "Don't worry, it's a known fact that women prioritise relationships above all else and men prioritise their purpose."

"Still makes me feel bad," Greg commented. "But you're right. There is a part of me that knows that until I am fully living my purpose, the relationship won't work."

"Then you are doing the right thing," Lisa commented. "You're an Atlantean. Inventing new sources of energy is part of what you are meant to do, it's within your soul. Follow that, and everything else will fall into place."

Greg thought about the memories he'd had of Atlantis, of his life there with Velvet, and he realised that he'd never truly appreciated how beautiful their life was, how blessed they were to have each other, to have abundance in their work and health, and to have lived in such a beautiful place. Until Velvet's vision of the end, and her untimely demise and the loss of their child, they had lived a blissful existence. But he could suddenly see that unless he let go of the pain and anguish he'd felt over losing her, and then carried with him ever since, he was never going to experience that blissful existence again.

He took his mug to the sink, and washed up a few dishes, lost in his thoughts while Julie and Lisa chatted quietly behind him.

He hadn't been prioritising his relationship with Violet, and though he knew he needed to focus on his purpose, perhaps it wouldn't be a bad idea to ask Lisa to finally release and heal his trauma from that lifetime, and then from the subsequent lifetimes he'd experienced without Velvet.

He was ready.

*　*　*

Gold watched the fire crackling in the hearth, and allowed himself become mesmerised by the dancing flames. He hadn't been on Earth for long, yet the pull of his Flame was so strong, he could not focus on anything other than the fact that he was desperate to see her, hear her voice, touch her skin.

"Gold, just go to her," Jaron said, walking into the living room. "She came to you, she told you to come. If you don't go soon, she might give up waiting and try to go find you."

Gold shook his head. "No, she wouldn't do that, she wouldn't leave Earth, leave her children."

"But she might well be wondering where on Earth you are. Go to her. You're certainly not going to be able to accomplish anything else until you've at least seen her."

When Gold didn't move immediately, Jaron sighed. "Would you like me to come with you?"

Gold smiled at his friend. "I would appreciate the company, yes."

"Let's go then, while it's still light out, it's a nice walk."

"Now?"

"Yes, my friend. Now. Go get some decent clothes on, sort your hair out, then get back down here in five minutes."

Gold nodded, feeling like he had no choice. His friend was clearly fed up with his morose behaviour. He followed the instructions, and just a few minutes later returned to where his friend waited.

Jaron looked him up and down and nodded. "Yeah, you'll do. Let's go."

Gold frowned, and checked himself in the hallway mirror before following Jaron out the door. He thought he looked more than acceptable. He sighed. What did it matter? Appearances had never really bothered him or Starlight. They loved each other's souls, not their good looks. Yet some feelings of human insecurity had already taken hold.

Starlight's home really wasn't very far, only a twenty-five minute walk. And the closer they got, the more Gold could feel her presence. He found himself getting short of breath, and he was unsure if it was from the exertion or from her proximity.

When they were just a couple of houses away, Gold stopped in his tracks.

"What if she doesn't recognise me? What if she still wants to be with her husband? What if I'm too late? What if-"

"Is one of the worst questions in history. Just get yourself to her front door and see what happens. Goodness me, Gold, you're like a teenager! You're an Elder of Earth, why not start acting like one?"

Gold sighed and stood a little straighter. "I know you're right, I just have so many fears. I mean, she left me there, then when she could have returned, she refused. Why does she want me here now?"

"Maybe because she is not full of fear, but full of hope for a new world to flourish. Now quit philosophising and get over there and ring the bloody doorbell."

Gold nodded, and before he could question and doubt himself further. He marched over to her house, went straight up to the front door, and knocked loudly, hurting his knuckles in the process.

He was inspecting his painful hand when the door swung inwards, and he found himself face to face with Gareth, Starlight's husband.

"Yes?" he asked.

Gold hadn't considered what he would do if Starlight didn't answer the door herself. "Um, is Star- I mean, Sarah here?"

Gareth frowned, then called over his shoulder. "Sarah! Someone at the door."

"Who is it?" Gold heard her yell back.

"Who are you?" Gareth asked.

Gold hadn't expected that, either. How could he say his name was Gold? It sounded ridiculous. "Um, Jaron," he stammered, figuring his old friend wouldn't mind him borrowing his name. But why couldn't Starlight sense it was him? He'd been able to sense her a couple of miles away.

"Jaron!" Gareth yelled over his shoulder.

"Who? I don't know any Jarons!"

Gareth frowned at Gold. "What do you want, mate? How do you know Sarah?"

"Um, we're old friends, but it's been a while, she might have forgotten," Gold faltered, seeing Gareth's face shut down.

"Well, she doesn't know you, and she's busy right now, so perhaps you need to go."

He stepped back and began to close the door, but a surge of strength, which came from a place that Gold had not accessed in quite some time, rose to the surface and he stopped the door from being closed.

"Please just ask her to come to the door. I know she will recognise me if she sees me."

Gareth looked at Gold's hand in the way of the door and sighed. "Wait here."

He went into the house, and Gold strained to hear their conversation. What felt like a lifetime later, he saw Starlight, his Flame, coming toward him. She stopped a couple of steps away and frowned at him.

"Who are you?" she asked. There was no recognition on her face.

"Starlight?" Gold whispered. "It's me, Gold."

Sarah gasped and stepped back in shock, a hand to her heart. "Gold?" she whispered.

He nodded, and she stepped closer, peering at his face, which was young and unlined, and quite different to how she would have remembered. He was so nervous that he felt his right eye begin to twitch.

Sarah smiled then. "Gold," she said with more certainty. "You came."

He nodded again, unable to form any words from his jumbled thoughts. Her smile, her scent, and the heat he could feel from her body were all rendering him incapable of coherence.

She glanced over her shoulder. "Now isn't the best time, and Gareth seems to be in a bad mood. Where are you staying? I can come and see you while the kids are in school."

Gold managed to give her Jaron's address, and she smiled and reached out to touch his hand. A thousand memories of their unions flashed through Gold's mind, and he smiled back.

"I will see you tomorrow," he whispered.

"Tomorrow," Sarah echoed, her smile deepening.

It took a lot of effort for Gold to walk away, and allow her to close the door, but he knew that it wouldn't be long before he got to see his Flame again.

He joined Jaron where he was sat on a nearby wall.

"Well?" Jaron asked.

"She's coming to visit tomorrow," Gold said, still feeling dazed.

"See? That wasn't so hard, was it?" Jaron said, getting up and stretching. "Let's get home and have some hot chocolate. There's a documentary on TV tonight I want to see."

Gold nodded and followed his friend, already thinking about the next day.

He couldn't wait.

*   *   *

Violet looked around the packed room in amazement. Of her smaller speaking events so far, this was the busiest one yet. The room in Spirit's Child couldn't have held any more people. The lady who ran the shop loved Violet's book, so she had told everyone that Violet was visiting.

They were an interactive audience, and Violet had enjoyed the questions that were asked. Though she didn't always feel like she had answers for all of them, it was fun to explore different ideas. After her talk, there had been a long line of people waiting to buy her book and talk to her.

"I just want to thank you, for tonight," a shy-looking lady said as she held out a book for Violet to sign. "I walked in here this evening not believing in anything. Thinking I was alone in this world. And now, after hearing you speak, I believe in something. I believe that there's a reason for everything that is happening, and I don't feel alone now." She smiled, tears in her eyes. "I really look forward to reading your book."

Violet's eyes filled with tears, and she got up and went around the table to the lady and embraced her. She hugged her and said to her quietly, "I'm so pleased you now believe. The Angels are with you always, you are never, ever alone."

The woman nodded and they smiled at each other. Violet wiped her eyes and then sat back down to sign a book for the woman. As she always did, she wrote a little message on the front page. She handed the book to the woman, who was now crying openly, and hoped that her book and her message would strengthen the woman's belief that she was loved.

It was a busy evening, and Violet even ended up signing books for most of the staff, who were fans of the book already.

By the time she'd finished, her hand was aching and her cheeks hurt from smiling.

"I guess you won't have had dinner yet?"

Violet looked up to see a guy standing by the smudge stick stand smiling at her. She shook her head. "I had some snacks before, but I'm starving now," she said.

"Would you like to go to dinner? I know a great Italian nearby," he said.

Violet thought back to the books she'd signed, and put a name and a face together. "Thank you, David, that does sound nice," She was about to turn down his offer, in favour of getting the taxi back to Robert's house, when she changed her mind and decided to go with the flow. "So, yeah, why not? Lead the way."

David smiled, and he led her out of the shop. She called goodbye to the ladies, and they headed out into the darkness. The ground was wet from an earlier thunderstorm, and Violet was glad it had stopped raining, as she had been dressed for the sunshine.

She followed David to his car, wondering how sensible it had been to agree to go to dinner with a complete stranger, but he had asked several thoughtful questions during her talk, and he had an energy, an aura, around him that made Violet feel at ease, like she could trust him implicitly.

They drove to the Italian restaurant in silence, which didn't seem all that nearby to Violet, but then in America, everything seemed to be spread out over big distances.

David parked the car outside the restaurant, then got out and went around to open the door for Violet. She was a little surprised, most guys just didn't do that anymore.

"Thank you," she said, getting out of the car. They walked to the entrance of the restaurant, and stepped inside to the podium where the greeter awaited them.

"Table for two?"

David nodded, and the greeter led them to a cosy booth, in a quieter section, away from a big party who appeared to be celebrating a birthday.

"May I get you something to drink?"

"Just water for me, please," Violet said.

"A Sprite, please," David said.

They settled into the booth, opposite each other, and Violet suddenly felt really tired. She wondered again why she had agreed to have dinner; she would have been better off getting an early night in preparation for the event the following day.

"I know you must be quite tired, it was a busy event tonight, but I'm glad you agreed to have dinner with me," David said, uncannily echoing her thoughts.

Violet smiled and picked up the menu. "Thank you for the invite, I am actually starving. I would have probably just gone back and had some bad mac and cheese before passing out, so you've saved me."

David chuckled. "You're welcome. I really enjoyed your talk tonight, and I look forward to reading your book. To be honest, it's not normally my thing, Angels and Faeries. I only came into the shop to buy a gift for a friend, but I saw the poster for tonight and felt compelled to attend."

"I guess you were meant to then."

"Yeah, I think I was." David stared into Violet's eyes and she sensed his energy shifting. Not many men had looked at her in that way, and despite the way things were with Greg, Violet didn't feel repelled by his gaze. Instead, she felt curious.

"What's good to eat here?" she asked, breaking eye contact and scanning the menu.

"I love the pizza, but the pasta dishes are pretty good too."

Violet nodded and saw a pizza with her favourite toppings on it. She set the menu down, and a few moments later, a waiter arrived with their drinks and an order pad.

They ordered their food, and then David asked her some questions about the Retreat. She launched into a description of the different themes they had for the Twin Flames, and some of the success stories.

When the food arrived, Violet stopped talking and dove into the pizza, feeling utterly famished.

"And your husband doesn't mind you touring the States on your own?"

Violet saw his gaze resting on her wedding ring, and smiled at him. "We fully support each other in our missions. He wanted me to follow mine, and this trip just seemed to all come together so effortlessly." She sighed. "But we're also giving each other a bit of space. He is trying to figure out his purpose, and he thought it would be better if we didn't communicate for a while, so we could both focus."

David raised an eyebrow. "And how's that working for you?"

Violet laughed. "Not great, I suppose. I mean, I have done several events, made some wonderful connections, and I feel like word is spreading about my book, which I do believe is the main part of my purpose here."

"But?"

Violet smiled at his intuitive ability to read her. "But I miss him. And I wonder what he's doing. And whether we will be together again soon."

David nodded. "It's tough when you find the one you love and it just doesn't quite work out."

"Well, I wouldn't say it hasn't worked out," Violet said, frowning. "Is that what you get from what I've said?"

David frowned too. "If it was working, why would you need space from each other?"

Violet picked up a slice of pizza and bit into it, thinking. She chewed slowly, then swallowed. "I suppose it doesn't seem strange because I have met so many Flames who are separated for so many different reasons. I don't see separation as meaning it's not working. I see it as a breather while both parties are working out what they need or want, or are healing, or letting go of something."

"Maybe what you need to let go of is each other."

Violet continued to eat her pizza, and wanted to protest his words, but for some reason they made so much sense to her.

She needed to let go of Greg. Otherwise she would never focus on her mission. She wouldn't be able to help as many Earth Angels, because instead of helping them, she would be in the woods, tucked away from the world.

Violet sipped her water, feeling both torn to shreds, and oddly relieved.

"Perhaps you're right," she said softly.

David smiled and reached out to touch her hand. She felt a spark when he did, a feeling of attraction, which surprised her.

"Enough about me," she said. "Tell me something about yourself, what do you do?"

David smiled at the change in subject. "I design computer programmes primarily, but I've been working on some personal projects, and well, one of them has gotten quite a lot of attention."

"Oh, what is it?" Violet asked, not sure if she would even understand it, her computing skills were pretty basic.

"I've just designed a machine that is capable of recording your dreams."

Violet choked on the sip of water she had just taken. "What?" she sputtered.

"Are you okay?"

She took another sip and nodded. "Yes, I'm fine. But what do you mean? It can record dreams?"

"Exactly that. I can hook someone up to my computer, and when they sleep their dreams can be visually recorded, and then replayed the next day. It's still in testing mode, but I've tried it, it works."

Violet's eyes were wide and she wasn't sure what to say. "Um, that's amazing. When did you create it?"

"A few weeks ago. I forget the date, but hang on, there's an article online about it, here." David found the article on his phone and handed the small device to Violet. She scanned the words, and picked out the date. It was the same date as their manifestation circle. She was sure of it.

It had worked.

"This really is amazing," she said calmly, while inside she was in shock.

"Thanks." David took the phone back and put it in his pocket. "Would you like to get some dessert?"

Violet shook her head. "I really ought to get a taxi back to my friend's place."

"No need, I can drop you off, save you some money."

Violet smiled. "Thank you, I'd appreciate that."

David insisted on paying for dinner, and they made their way out to the car. Violet got Robert's address out of her bag and David put it into the SatNav. Aside from the robotic directions, they drove in silence.

Violet's mind was whirling in chaos. She was blown away by David being the inventor of what they had manifested, and question after question ran through her head. How could she be attracted to someone else? How could she be considering letting go of Greg? Her husband? Her Twin Flame? Since their meeting that day in La Rochelle, when she fell off the rocks, she had never considered being with another man.

But she was drawn to David in a way she couldn't explain. Was it because of the connection through the dream recorder? Because she had helped in some way? She felt completely at ease with him, and they were able to talk as though they had known each other for years. Based on what he did for a living and his appearance, Violet guessed that he was a Starperson. Not that she had mentioned that to him. He was very open minded, but also very new to the spiritual stuff. Telling someone who had invited you out to dinner that they were an alien in a former life was perhaps not the best idea.

They arrived outside Robert's home, and Violet unbuckled her seatbelt. She smiled at David. "Thank you so much for coming to the event, buying my book and then taking me out to dinner. I really appreciate it, it was lovely to meet you."

"It was my pleasure, I enjoyed every minute."

He leaned forward a little, and without thinking, Violet leaned toward him too. She closed her eyes and when their lips met, she felt a spark of recognition, of knowing him. Their kiss deepened, and lasted for several moments before some common sense kicked in and she pulled away. She blinked at him in the semi-darkness. "I'm sorry, I don't know what came over me," she said.

"I can feel the connection too. I've been able to feel it all evening."

Violet nodded. "It's strong. But it doesn't change the fact that I'm married."

David leaned back in his seat. "I know, I'm sorry. I just needed to see if you felt it too."

"I do, and that's confusing. But I love Greg, that hasn't changed."

They sat in silence for a few moments, and Violet sighed. "I should go."

"Can I see you again?"

Violet bit her lip, then nodded. She told him where she was doing the event the following day.

"I can take you there," he said.

"I'd like that." Violet opened the car door and let herself out. David waited until she had reached the front door and stepped inside before driving away. She closed the door and then leaned against it.

What had she done?

Chapter Fifteen

Emerald watched her friend, and could see all of the emotions flitting across her face, but the Angel felt that by bringing David into the picture, they had indeed made it possible for Violet to let go. Her heart ached when she saw the confusion in Violet's expression. She was clearly wrestling with the feelings she was having for this perfect stranger. Though actually, he wasn't a stranger at all.

"Are you impressed I managed to track down Bk?" Mica asked.

Emerald smiled at her Flame. "Yes, it was a stroke of good fortune that he happens to live in Arizona. I can see that Violet feels a deep connection to him. That will happen after spending so many years together at the Academy."

"Do you think anything will happen between them?"

Emerald shrugged. "I don't know. It's possible. Though Bk isn't entirely over his previous relationship either."

"Yeah, that's a pretty tough deal, having your wife leave you for another woman."

"He's such a lovely guy though, he and Violet would make quite a wonderful couple," Emerald mused, hoping that her friend would forgive her for meddling with her love life and her emotions.

"Yes, they would, even with Velvet's history of not getting

on with Starpeople."

"Are you guys busy?"

Mica and Emerald looked up from their conversation to see Pearl standing there.

"Pearl! How are you? What brings you here to our headquarters?"

Pearl smiled. "I wanted to check on Gold, and I felt it would be easier to do it here than at the lake. I don't wish to raise any suspicions about how we are meddling with the timeline. Pallas and the other Elders are still in the dark on this. Also, I just wanted to see how things were going. I haven't had an update in a while."

"Ah, sorry about that. Gold has been to see Starlight, but they were unable to talk at any length. Last time we checked they were going to meet up to talk. And everything else is happening according to our strategies, so hopefully we are still very much on track."

"What about Aragonite? Has he found Cotton?"

Emerald frowned and looked over at Mica, who shrugged.

"Actually, we haven't seen him in the water, so I'm not sure. We will have to look for him and check. He walked onto Earth in his own body, so he should be easy enough to find."

Pearl nodded. "That's all good to hear. Though I still occasionally have twinges of doubt over what we are doing, I do feel it is all ultimately for the best of all humankind. Even with the slight hiccup we had."

Emerald smiled at the mild way she referenced the darkness and chaos they had managed to avoid.

"We're sure that it is too. With our nudges, more Earth Angels will Awaken, and therefore more humans will also Awaken, and the Golden Age will be a reality."

"It will be quite a miraculous feat. As we have seen, it doesn't take much to shift the world onto an entirely different path, and I fear that without this burst of light from the mass Awakenings, the whole world could still be plunged into the darkness, never to resurface."

Emerald felt compelled to hug the Angel in front of her. She got up and wrapped her arms and wings around her, and Pearl did the same in return.

Within their cocoon of feathers, Emerald whispered, "I have such faith in Violet. I have not had this faith in the past, and I have always been wrong. So now I choose to have faith that her presence on Earth will stop the world wars, will bring love to those who feel unloved, bring companionship to those who feel they are all alone, and bring faith and belief to those who have none. And with Gold there on Earth too, I cannot imagine that the Golden Age will not come about now."

With tears in her eyes, Pearl whispered back. "Thank you, Angel. I believe you. I have faith too. My Flame is also doing magnificent work, he has already helped and Awakened millions. I know that their energies on Earth will make all the difference. My heart just hurts every time I must welcome souls home from Earth who have left due to anger, lack and conflict."

"I know. But remain strong, Angel. They need us to be that for them." The women embraced for a while longer, then released each other.

"I must return to the gates, I hope you find Aragonite, and that he is okay. He has not been to Earth before, and I don't know if he arranged for any help when he got there, he left very suddenly."

"We will find him, fear not."

"Peace, love and light be with you," Pearl said.

"And with you," Mica replied.

The Angel left, and Emerald turned to Mica. "I feel a bit concerned about Aragonite now, why haven't we seen him in our viewing? He couldn't have found Cotton yet, we would have known about it from watching Greg."

Mica frowned and turned to his basin. "Let's find him."

* * *

Greg carried the tray of mugs carefully up the stairs, and could hear the chatter of his friends in the workshop room. He entered the dimly lit space and set the tray down in the middle.

"Thanks, Greg," Beatrice said, picking up a mug of coffee. "I think we all have something that we want to focus on."

~ 135 ~

"Great," Greg said, picking up his own mug and cradling it in his hands. "How shall we structure it? Should we just take it in turns? Say out loud to the group what we want to manifest, in as much detail as we can, and then the group focusses on that for ten minutes? Then move onto the next?"

Julie shrugged. "Sounds good to me. Though last time we all apparently fell asleep whilst focusing. Should we set a timer for ten minutes?"

"Good idea," Lisa said, getting her phone out of her bag. "I'll set a timer."

"I still can't believe we actually manifested a dream recording machine," Amy said. "It's a shame it didn't just materialise right in front of us. That would have been amazing."

"I think we would have passed out in shock," Lisa commented.

"Okay," Greg said, moving the tea tray to the centre of their circle, just as Violet had done the first time they tried the method. "Who wants to go first?"

"I'll go first," Amy said. "I would like to manifest perfect health for my mum. She's been quite ill recently, and they're doing tests to find out what's wrong, as they're not sure right now. I'd like for her to see me get married to Joe next year and also see her grandchildren grow up when we have them."

"Those are good visuals," Julie said. "I can see your mum looking healthy, and playing with two kids."

"Okay, shall we make a start? Lisa, can you set the timer?"

"Yep," Lisa said, pressing the screen of her phone. The group then all focussed on the tray, and fell silent.

When the timer sounded, Greg blinked in surprise. "Has it really been ten minutes?"

The others looked shocked too. "I swear that was like thirty seconds," Amy said.

Lisa picked up her phone and switched off the alarm. "It was ten minutes. Do you think that's long enough? We seem to enter some kind of timeless zone while we do this."

"I'm sure it's fine. Besides, if we do any longer than that, we won't get through everyone's manifestations before Beatrice needs to go."

"Okay," Lisa said, resetting the timer. "Who's next?"

"I would like to find a harmonious relationship with someone who loves me exactly as I am, and who loves my children as if they were his own," Julie said. "Can you all imagine me with him?"

Everyone nodded, and Lisa hit the start button on her screen, before they all fell silent again.

After what seemed like a few seconds, but was in reality about eight minutes, Greg was startled by a loud hammering on the front door. The rest of the group were also jolted back into awareness. Greg frowned. "I wonder who that could be, is anyone expecting anyone?"

The women all shook their heads, and Greg stood up, his limbs aching from sitting so still on the floor. He headed down the stairs, curious to see who the late-night visitor was.

"Is Cotton there?"

Greg frowned at the man with long brown dreadlocks and piercing amber-coloured eyes, who looked – and smelled – as though he had not washed in weeks. "Cotton?" he repeated.

"Blue Cotton. That's probably not her name now, but she was the Professor of Patience at the Earth Angel Training Academy."

Greg's eyes widened. He remembered Violet and Julie talking about who she had been at the Academy. But how did this complete stranger know who she was before and where she was now?

"Who are you?" he asked.

"Aragonite?"

Greg turned to see Julie standing behind him, her hand over her mouth. He looked back at the stranger, and saw him nod, tears filling his eyes. "It's me, Blue."

Greg stepped aside to allow the man into the house, and Julie approached, in disbelief at the sight before her. When they touched, Greg could almost see the flare of energy that was sparked by their contact.

"How are you here? You said you were going to another galaxy, to other planets," Julie said, tears now streaming down her face.

"I did. Then once the job was finished, I returned to the Angelic Realm. But I couldn't stay there any longer, I had to come and find you."

Julie nodded, and Greg averted his gaze while they kissed. He closed the front door, and headed to the kitchen to put the kettle on. He felt that Aragonite might appreciate a hot drink, as well as a shower and some clean clothes.

When he returned to the front room, Julie and Aragonite were still embracing, and speaking in hushed tones.

"Would you like a drink? And a shower?" Greg asked.

The two turned to look at him and Aragonite chuckled. "Yes, please, that sounds amazing. I've been walking and hitching for a week, and I know I absolutely stink."

"I'll get some clean clothes out and a towel. The trousers might be a bit short on you though."

"That would be great, it's no problem. May I shower first?"

Greg nodded and motioned for him to follow him up the stairs, and Julie went to the kitchen to make the drinks.

After showing Aragonite how to use the shower, and sorting out some clean clothes, Greg went downstairs to help Julie.

He found her crying quietly next to the kettle.

"Hey, are you okay?" Greg asked.

Julie looked up and smiled through her tears. "Yes, I just can't believe it. Aragonite is my Flame, and I never thought I would see him again. I guess I'm just in shock."

Greg nodded. "Especially seeing as we were in the middle of manifesting you a man."

"Oh my goodness! We were! That is just crazy. Do you really think we called him here?"

Greg shrugged. "It's an incredible coincidence, that's for sure. The others are going to freak out when we tell them."

Julie laughed and continued making the hot drinks. "They are."

The two of them carried the mugs upstairs, and entered the workshop room. Greg could hear the shower still running.

"Who was it?" Amy asked. "And who's in the shower?"

Julie and Greg sat down and handed out the mugs, then Julie spoke. "It was my Twin Flame."

There were gasps of surprise. "What?" Lisa asked. "I thought he wasn't coming to earth? That he had gone to other planets?"

"He did, but when the work was done, he returned to the Angelic Realm, then he came here to find me. He said he couldn't bear to be apart from me any longer."

"That is amazing," Amy said. "And he arrives while we're manifesting a man for you? What are the chances? Seriously?"

"Can we manifest mine now please?" Lisa said with a laugh.

"Shall we ask him if he wants to join the circle?" Greg asked Julie. "Or do you think he'd prefer to rest? He looked pretty exhausted."

"I'll go and ask him in a moment."

They drank their tea and chatted until Julie heard the shower switch off, and then a few minutes later, footsteps approaching the workshop room.

"Hello?" Greg turned to see Aragonite peering into the room, and he waved for him to come in.

Julie moved to the side a little to make space for him to join them, and she handed him a cup of tea.

"We're having a manifestation circle. Did you want to join us? Apparently it's what they used to do in Atlantis."

Aragonite drank the tea then nodded. "Sure, sounds fun. What exactly do we have to do?"

"We're taking it in turns to state what we would like to manifest, then as a group, we're all focusing on it. Amy and I have already had our turns, so it's Lisa's next."

Lisa smiled at Julie and blushed a little. She said out loud the kind of relationship she wanted to manifest, then they all closed their eyes and visualised it.

Greg wondered if they were about to get another knock on the door.

* * *

"How's it going?"

Violet looked up and squinted into the sunlight. She saw

Robert smiling at her from where he stood by the pool. She splashed her feet in the water and nodded.

"Everything's good, just absorbing some sun while I can."

Robert sat down next to her and dangled his feet into the pool. "I can't imagine being somewhere cold now, I need the vitamin D too much."

"I struggle sometimes," Violet said. "When the cold and damp gets into my bones, it's hard to get anything done."

Robert chuckled. "I can picture you wrapped up in a blanket, a mug of tea in hand, while it rains outside."

Violet smiled. "That's pretty much what it's like in the UK. Wet and cold." She sighed and tilted her face to the sun. "This feels so good."

"Yes it does."

There was nothing but the sound of the pool filter whirring and birds singing in a nearby tree for a few moments.

"I read your book," Violet said. "I had no idea you have been through so much, it was a real eye-opener."

Robert smiled. "It's been a helluva ride, that's for sure."

"I went home once," Violet said softly. "I couldn't face being here, so I left."

"But you came back? Like I did?" Robert asked.

Violet smiled wryly. "After a fashion, yes. It took me a while to figure out that I needed to be here, that I couldn't just take the easy way out."

"Ain't that the truth?"

Violet remembered a passage from his book. "Do you know what it is yet? The important thing you still need to do?"

Robert was thoughtful for a moment. "Every time I think I've got it figured out, it seems to change. I thought it was writing my book, sharing my experiences, changing people's views on death. But now, I think perhaps there is something even bigger than that. Otherwise, why am I still here? My illness should have taken me long ago."

Violet nodded. "I'm still working out exactly what it is I still have to do. I think I'm following my path, but then," she thought of David, "the Universe seems to be throwing me curveballs."

Robert chuckled. "I've had my fair share of those."

"Have you heard of the Crystal Child, Kasey? She spoke at the Angel Conference I spoke at a couple of weeks ago."

"No, doesn't ring a bell."

"Her story is as amazing as yours. She was in hospital, dying of cancer, when on Christmas Day, she says an Angel came and healed her. Since then, she has been healing others, and sharing her miraculous story." Violet shook her head. "Extraordinary girl. She knew me before we had met, and healed me of the broken heart I had been carrying since I went home to the stars and came back. Also healed my nerves. I can speak quite easily to large audiences now."

"She sounds like quite a gal."

"I need to connect you two, I think you would get on really well."

Robert nodded. "I'd like that. Now, I need a drink, you make sure you don't cook out here, okay?"

Violet smiled and nodded. "Okay." She watched her friend retreat into the cool of the house, and she pondered what might come of bringing Robert and the Crystal Child together.

* * *

For the third day in a row, Gold answered the door to his Flame, his heart beating fast and his stomach filled with butterflies.

"Gold," she said, making his heart thud faster. She stepped into Jaron's living room. "It's a good thing I work for myself from home," Sarah commented. "I would never normally get this many days off."

"What about your husband? Does he know?"

"Of course not. Gareth wouldn't understand that I have been meeting with my Flame. And despite the fact that we have done nothing but talk, he would automatically assume that I had cheated on him." She sighed. "I don't want to deal with that kind of drama right now."

"So, we've skirted around the issue for the last few days, but don't you think we ought to figure out what's going on?"

Sarah frowned. "What do you mean?"

"You called me here, you told me to come to Earth. To be

with you."

Sarah shook her head. "I told you to come to Earth, but I never said it was to be with me. In fact, I didn't really say why. I just hoped you would trust me."

"But..." Gold thought back to the messages he'd received. She was right, she never said to come to be with her. That had been his own assumption, his own hope.

"Why am I here then? If not to be with you?"

"You're here to raise the vibration of Earth in preparation of the shift that will take us into the Golden Age. We're so close now, but we need the Elders on Earth to come together, join forces to make it happen."

"So you still do not wish to be with me, even as I stand before you now?"

Sarah sighed. "Of course I wish to be with you, but our union is not the purpose of your return to Earth, the Golden Age is."

"But surely our union will play a part in raising the vibration? Our joined energies are incredibly powerful."

Sarah reached out to touch Gold's hand. "I love you, Gold. And I know you can feel that, deep in your heart and soul. But we have jobs to do and to do them means setting aside our own needs and desires, and focusing on the needs of the collective."

Sarah stood up. "I feel I should leave, I will return when you feel able to move forward with the plan. You have my mobile number, get Jaron to text me."

Gold stood up too, and despite wanting to respect her wishes, his desire to breathe in her scent and kiss her lips were too strong to resist. He stepped forward and wrapped his arms around her waist, pulling her toward him.

"Gold, what are you doing?" she asked softly.

Without a word, he leaned down and a moment before their lips touched, she closed her eyes, then he closed his.

The feeling of being home, of being utterly calm and peaceful washed over him, and he deepened the kiss. Sarah responded, and he pulled her body even closer to his.

After a few moments, she put her hand on his chest and gently pushed him away.

"Gold, this is not why I asked you to come to Earth. I still need to keep my family together, I still have a purpose that involves my children and husband. I'm sorry that you feel I misguided you, but the world needs you right now. More than I do."

Gold sighed. "But I need you. You have no idea how dreadful it has felt, being in the Fifth Dimension without you. I miss you so much, Starlight. My existence is dark and empty without your light."

Sarah sighed. "I miss you too, but this is important, Gold. It won't be long before we are reunited for all of eternity. But right now, we have missions to complete."

She leaned forward to kiss him, and it took all his strength to not pick her up and carry her up the stairs to his room. When she pulled away, he kept his eyes closed, and dropped his arms.

"I'll see you soon," she said softly.

Gold didn't open his eyes again until long after she had left.

Chapter Sixteen

"Huh, I really didn't see that one coming," Emerald commented, after watching Starlight reject Gold. "Starlight really has got a lot of secrets up her sleeve."

Mica nodded in agreement with his Flame. "I believed that she called Gold to Earth for a reunion. I'm as shocked as you."

"Poor Gold, it took so much for him to find the courage to return to Earth, and now his only reason for going there has been taken away. Do you think he will stay?"

They watched Jaron consoling the Elder for a while.

"I hope he does, Starlight clearly needed him to be there. And it seems to be related to the shift we are all working on. After all, things only improved on the timeline when Gold got to Earth."

"What else are we working on?" Emerald asked, shifting her attention to another place. "I'm so pleased that Aragonite made it to the Retreat in the end. To think he had been homeless and hitching rides from the moment he arrived. I wish he had stopped long enough to arrange help from someone."

Mica smiled. "I guess he just couldn't wait a moment longer. It was pretty brilliant timing, him turning up just as they were manifesting a soulmate for Julie."

"Do you think they now really believe in the process?" Emerald asked. "Olivine seems to think that their belief in the ability to manifest that which they focus on with intent will be a huge part of the shift. It will see more people focusing on the things they want, raising their vibration, and aligning with their desires and their highest good."

"It makes sense, and yes, I think they do believe. Whether they still will if not everything they tried to manifest comes true, we will have to see."

Emerald frowned. "What won't come true?"

"Amy's mother is ready to come home. Her illness will be sudden and severe, and she will be coming home to the Angelic Realm soon."

"Oh, poor Amy," Emerald said, her heart breaking for the sweet Angel. "She will be devastated. She is so close to her mother."

"I hope she will understand, and know that her mother will be with her in spirit during all those events she said she wanted her to experience."

A tear trickled down Emerald's cheek, and Mica reached over to smooth it away. "I know that you can feel her pain already, but she will get through it. Joe will help her, as will her friends."

Emerald nodded and tried to smile. "I can remember what it feels like, to lose a loved one. It must be the hardest thing I ever experienced as a human."

Mica sighed. "Believe me, I know it is. When I lost you, I just had no reason to live anymore. You were my anchor, keeping me on Earth. Velvet and Laguz did their best to ground me, to keep me going, but it all just seemed pointless. I was so happy when I realised that I was on the Other Side. I hadn't intended to get into a car accident, but I certainly wasn't sad to leave Earth."

"I wasn't happy to be back here," Emerald admitted.

Mica frowned. "What? You didn't want to come home? Why didn't you choose to return then?"

"Because I was just so tired of struggling. I wanted to be with you, so badly, but the idea of struggling on in human form was just too overwhelming. So when Gold asked if I wanted to return to Earth, or to stay, I chose to stay. But I felt like I made the choice because I was just too exhausted to go back. Not because I really wanted to come home."

Mica was quiet for a while. "That makes me feel better. That you didn't want to leave me. At the time, I didn't understand why you just gave up. I didn't realise how tired you were." He reached over to touch her hand. "I'm sorry, my sweet Flame. I should have taken better care of you."

Emerald shook her head. "You did everything you possibly could. You really couldn't have done more. I'm just glad that we never have to separate ever again. Now then," she said, wiping away her tears and returning her gaze to the basin. "Who are we going to try and reunite now?"

*   *   *

"Greg?"

"Lisa? What is it?"

He listened to her sobbing for a few moments, and his heart began to thud. "Lisa? Are you okay? What's going on?"

"It's Missy, she, she-" Lisa dissolved into sobs again.

"Where are you? Are you at home?" Greg was already pulling on a jacket and heading to the door while he waited for her to stop crying long enough to answer.

"Yes."

"I'll be there in ten minutes."

He hung up, and got ready to leave. He had been about to eat, but he couldn't leave her in such a state by herself. He slipped his shoes on, locked the door, and ran to the van. As he drove down the lane, he wondered if Missy had already gone home, or if she was about to.

When he arrived at Lisa's flat, the door was ajar. He pushed it open gently, calling out her name.

When there was no answer, he stepped in, and found Lisa in a heap on the floor.

"Oh, Lisa," he said, moving to her side. He knelt on the floor beside her and gathered her up in his arms.

While she sobbed, he glanced around the room. His gaze settled on a vet's bill on the coffee table. Missy had already gone.

"I'm so sorry, Lisa. I'm so, so sorry. Missy was an amazing dog."

Her sobbing got louder, and Greg just held her tightly to his chest. A tear slid down his own cheek. Lisa's grief was triggering unexpressed grief buried deep inside him. He took a deep breath and composed himself. She needed him to be strong and calm, not fall to pieces with her.

It was quite a while before her sobs began to calm, and her shoulders stopped shaking. He released his grip on her, and looked at her face. He smoothed a strand of hair from her wet cheek.

"I'm sorry," she choked out.

Greg shook his head. "Don't apologise. Missy was your best friend. And I'm so sorry."

Lisa's face crumpled again. "She was," she whispered. "It was so sudden. She was fine last night, then this morning she couldn't walk. I took her to the vets thinking that there was something they could do, but there wasn't." She shuddered.

Greg reached out and grabbed the box of tissues on the coffee table. He offered it to Lisa, and she pulled one out and blew her nose.

"I've had her for ten years. She's my family." She looked around the room. "Now I'll be all alone." She sniffled, and Greg pulled her close again.

"You're not alone. We're your family too. You always have a place at the retreat."

"Thank you."

They hugged for a while, and Greg became aware of his knees aching. "Let's get off this floor, and I'll put the kettle on."

"I'd rather something stronger. There's a bottle of whisky in the cupboard above the fridge."

Greg got up and pulled her up with him. He sat her down on the sofa, and then went to the kitchen to pour them both a drink. When he returned, he found Lisa hugging a framed photo of her and Missy.

He sat next to her and handed her the glass. "To Missy," he

said, clinking his glass against hers.

"To Missy," Lisa echoed.

They drank in silence for a while. Greg wasn't sure what else he could do or say to make Lisa feel any better, but he figured the fact she was no longer sobbing on the floor was a step forward.

"Have you heard from Violet?" Lisa asked suddenly.

Greg's heart thumped hard at hearing his wife's name. He shook his head. "I don't even know exactly where she is."

"I'm sorry," Lisa said. "It must be hard." She sighed. "Do you think you'll get back together?"

"I have no idea," Greg said. "She might have moved on already."

Lisa frowned. "Really? Do you think she has?"

Greg shrugged, feeling uncomfortable with the conversation. "It's possible. She's out in America, meeting lots of new people, it's possible she might meet someone she likes, who likes her too. She is pretty amazing."

Lisa put her hand on Greg's leg and squeezed. "I'm sorry, we don't have to talk about this."

"It's okay," Greg replied, even though he really didn't want to talk about it. He put his hand on hers.

"I've been dreaming about Atlantis again," Lisa said. "We spent a lot of time together under the water. It's pretty mad, really, that we have found each other again."

Greg smiled at Lisa. "What happened in your dream?"

Lisa blushed. "I remember you saving me from a shark, and afterwards, well, um,"

"What?"

"I kissed you," Lisa said.

Greg's eyes widened. Lisa leaned closer, and before he could fully process what was happening, her lips were on his. He kissed her back, but although it felt familiar, it didn't feel right. He pulled away, and Lisa opened her eyes and looked up at him.

"I'm sorry," he whispered. "I don't think this is right."

Lisa nodded. "I'm sorry too, I shouldn't have done that."

Greg shook his head. "It's okay. I would be lying if I said

I wasn't curious as well. I have felt very close to you recently. But there's something… missing."

Lisa smiled. "I know. I feel that too." She sighed. "I just thought, after the circle, when we were manifesting our desires, because Aragonite turned up, that perhaps I would find the man I wanted to manifest. Then I had the dream of us in Atlantis the night after the circle, and I thought that maybe it was you I was meant to be with. Can you forgive me?"

"There's nothing to forgive," Greg said, patting her knee. "I can understand how it might seem right. Deep connections like ours can feel confusing. The familiarity is persuasive." He sighed. "I'm sorry your man hasn't manifested yet, but perhaps Aragonite turning up at that exact moment was just a coincidence." He glanced up at the clock on the wall. "Julie will be back with the kids, I should let them know where I am, she worries."

"Go, I'll be okay now. Thank you for coming to rescue me again."

Greg set his half-finished drink on the coffee table. "Anytime. I mean that. If you need anything, call. And I'm sorry again about Missy."

Lisa looked down at the framed picture and nodded. "It will take some getting used to, not having her around. But maybe when I'm ready, I'll get a new furry soul to live with me."

"Didn't realise you liked hairy men," Greg remarked.

Lisa laughed. "Oh yeah, they're my favourite type."

Greg stood up, and Lisa followed him out to the door. They hugged, and he left.

When he reached the van and got inside, he put his fingers to his lips, and wondered if Violet was experiencing similar encounters with someone else.

Despite him telling her to move on, he realised that he wasn't really ready to lose her completely.

And he wasn't sure he ever would be.

* * *

Violet was getting ready to go out for dinner with David, and found herself sitting on her bed in Robert's home, twisting her wedding ring around her finger. She had finished her events in Arizona, and David had taken her to each one, listened attentively, and then taken her out for food afterwards, always insisting on paying.

They had talked for hours over the last three days, and she had found herself being drawn closer and closer to him.

And it was tearing her apart.

How could she be attracted to someone other than her Flame? Someone who was so different to her beautiful husband? And a Starperson no less? She had never really got on very well with Starpeople. Why did she think it would be a good match?

She could answer none of her own questions. But decided, in that moment, to take her ring off, and set it on the nightstand.

She wanted to be free to experience her last evening in Arizona with David, and see what came of it. She hadn't had any updates from home in a while, except the sad news of Amy's mother's illness, and so, for all she knew, Greg could be seeing other people too.

It seemed unlikely, but it was still a possibility.

She got up and finished dressing and applying her makeup and doing her hair. David would be picking her up in thirty minutes. He was taking her to a Mexican restaurant, and afterwards they were going to play crazy golf.

She got ready quickly, then went out to the living area, where Robert was watching a movie with his wife.

"I'll be quiet when I come in," she said to them. "I don't think I'll be too late, got to get to the airport early in the morning."

"Do you need a ride?" Robert asked.

"No, it's okay, David said he could take me. Have a lie in," Violet said with a smile. "I just wanted to say, in case I don't see you in the morning, how wonderful it was to meet you, and to thank you for inviting me to stay here, you've both been amazing. Thank you."

Robert got up to give her a hug, and she felt tears prickling behind her eyelids. She wondered why she felt so emotional over saying goodbye. She blinked rapidly and pulled away and smiled. "Keep in touch."

"You bet," Robert said.

Violet heard a knock at the door, and she dashed back to her room quickly to grab her bag before opening the front door.

David stood there with a stuffed bear in his hand.

"I figured that flowers would be a waste of time, but maybe you had room in your luggage for a lucky bear."

Violet smiled and accepted the gift. She gripped the soft fur in her hand, and her emotions welled up again. "It's lovely, thank you. And yes, it will fit, I'll put it in my hand luggage."

She stowed the bear safely in her room, before following David out to his car. The evening was still very warm, despite the sun having set a couple of hours before.

They got in the car, and David pulled away from the house. "All packed and ready to go?" he asked over the soft music playing on the radio.

"Yes, all packed. I'm looking forward to LA, but I'm sad to be leaving Arizona. It has been my favourite part of the trip so far."

David grinned. "Why is that?" he asked casually.

Violet chuckled. "Oh, I just really love the heat, and the cacti, that's all."

David nodded. "You're right. Nowhere else does cacti like Arizona."

Violet reached over to touch his leg. "Of course, I've really liked the people I met, too."

"Oh sure, there are some great people in Arizona."

"The best," Violet agreed.

They rode the rest of the way to the restaurant in silence, the radio playing softly. When they arrived, once again, David got out to open the door for Violet. She stepped out of the car, and happily took the arm he offered. They went into the restaurant and sat down at the table they were directed to. After ordering iced water for Violet, and a Sprite for himself, David reached over and took Violet's hands in his.

"I know we've only just met a few days ago, and you're leaving for LA tomorrow, and then England in a week, but I need to say this."

Violet's breath caught as she waited for him to continue.

"I feel as if I have known you forever. That our souls have been waiting for us to reunite. Now, I understand that you have met your Flame, but I feel as though we have a connection, one that could become a beautiful relationship."

Violet nodded, pleased that he felt the same way as she did, even though she felt guilty for feeling that way.

David rubbed his thumb over her finger where her ring should have been. "I know you are married to your Flame, and never imagined being with anyone else, but, well, I'm asking you that you consider the possibility. And that perhaps, when you finish your events in LA, instead of returning home to England, you come back here, to me."

Violet's eyes widened in shock. "You want me to stay?" she whispered.

"You have three months on your visa, right? You could stay another few weeks, and then when the visa is up, I could always come back with you."

When Violet didn't respond, he continued.

"I don't know how we would go about getting you a green card or anything, with you being married already, but even if it takes time to sort out, I'm sure it's all possible." He sighed. "I haven't been this happy in a very long time, and I just know that we could make each other so very happy." He squeezed her hands. "What are you thinking?"

Violet's mind was spinning crazily. He had told her what had happened with his wife, and she knew that he was still heartbroken that she had left him, and had apparently been lying about her sexuality for the duration of their marriage too. Violet hadn't realised he felt strongly enough about her to ask her to consider moving to a different continent to be with him. She thought of Greg, and her heart ached. Despite their break up, despite setting each other free to do what they wanted, she still wanted him, still loved him with everything she had.

But then she also found herself really liking the man sat in front of her, waiting for her response to his proposal. But did she – or could she – love him?

"Wow, I really don't know what to say," Violet said finally. "I mean, it's such a big step..."

The waiter appeared with their food, and Violet waited for the food to be placed on the table and for him to leave before she continued.

"You're right, despite all that's happened, I haven't ever considered being with someone else. But I do feel the connection to you, I do feel drawn to you in ways I can't explain, and I am curious about that."

In that moment, all Violet wanted was her Spiritual Sisters to be there, so she could ask them what she should do.

"I understand that you feel conflicted, separated or not, he's still your husband. And your Twin Flame. But maybe your path is supposed to lead elsewhere right now, with someone else."

Violet gasped, as the words of the crystal ball reader in New York City came flooding back to her in a rush. She had filed them away in the back of her mind, disbelieving their validity, but she realised in a flash that what he had predicted was in fact coming true.

"What is it?" David asked.

"In New York, I got a reading," Violet said, hardly believing that she was telling him. "And I was told that I would meet someone," her eyes were wide when they met his gaze. "Someone called David. That we would get married, and have a child." She shook her head. "I thought he was just crazy, and I disregarded it completely."

"Wow, he really said that?"

Violet nodded. "Yes. Unbelievable, isn't it?"

David shook his head. "No, I find it completely believable."

Violet raised an eyebrow. "Really? I would have thought it lacked any scientific or logical explanation."

"It may well do, but in this moment, I completely believe that you and I were meant to meet, and that a future together is entirely possible."

Violet took a deep breath, then sipped some of her water. She wondered if she should tell him about the manifestation circle, and how the dates coincided with his invention. It might just be a step too far though. She looked down at her plate. "We should eat, it's going cold."

David nodded and released her hand. They ate in silence for a few minutes.

"You don't have to make a decision immediately. Go to LA, do your events there, think about it. See how you feel in another week. And if you think it can work, call me, and I'll book you a flight back here."

Violet nodded. "Okay," she said slowly. "I can do that."

The smile on David's face melted her heart, and she knew that she could do much worse than to wake up every morning and see his face next to hers.

"No matter what happens though, I'm very glad to have met you," David said. "You've woken me up to the fact that life after divorce is possible, that it is okay to be happy again, and that I am capable of it."

Violet smiled at him. "Likewise. You've opened my eyes to the possibilities out in the world, and I am very thankful to you for that."

This time, they did have dessert, and by the time they left the restaurant, it was nearly eleven o'clock.

"Do you want to come back to mine tonight?" David whispered in her ear as they walked back to the car.

Violet stomach flipped, and her heart skipped a beat. Before she could think about it too hard, she nodded. "Yes, I do."

Chapter Seventeen

Greg leaned against the kitchen counter by the kettle, feeling too weary to stand up straight. He hadn't slept at all, and had tossed and turned until dawn finally broke.

"You're up early."

Greg jumped at Aragonite's voice behind him. He turned to look at the dishevelled Angel, who had been staying with Julie in the spare room since he'd arrived out of the blue.

Greg rubbed his eyes. "Couldn't sleep. Figured I should just get up and do something useful. How come you're up so early?"

Aragonite shrugged. "I felt the need to come downstairs." He sat down at the breakfast bar, and Greg got a second mug out and made them both strong coffees.

"So what's going on?" Aragonite asked after a few moments of silence. "What's happening with you and Velvet?"

Greg sat next to the Angel and frowned. He knew how to get straight to the point, it seemed. "We both felt it was necessary for her to go and follow her mission."

"Why can't she do that and still be with you?"

Greg thought for a moment. "I have no idea. To be honest, it felt like there were forces outside of ourselves encouraging us to separate. I miss her so much, and I am desperate to reach out to her. I have no idea where she is, or what she's doing, or even..." Greg's voice faltered. "Who she might be with."

"You're right."

"About what?" Greg asked, his heart beginning to pound.

"There were forces outside of you encouraging you to separate," Aragonite said. "But this is not information to be shared with anyone else. I'm telling you this, because, well, since meeting you, since reuniting with Blue, I think we might have been wrong."

Greg stared into the Angel's eyes. "We? Wrong? What are you talking about?"

Aragonite sighed. "When I was sorting out the rogue planets, I met the Angel of Destiny. She and I worked together to bring order and peace to those planets, and then she asked me to return and do the same for Earth. I created a team of Angels in the Angelic Realm, and we have been working to bring the world into the Golden Age. In order to do so, we had to make some decisions, and we had to… nudge people."

Greg's eyes widened as he comprehended the man's words. "You mean, there's a team of Angels up there, influencing people? Influencing me, and Violet? Making us separate?"

Aragonite nodded. "It seemed to be the best thing, considering the bigger picture. For you to have this period of separation. But I am doubtful of our decisions now. I don't see how keeping Flames apart can be a good thing for the world."

Greg stared down at his mug, trying to take in this new information. "So Starlight, that is, Sarah, knew about this? She knew that we were being forcibly separated, and yet she said nothing?"

Aragonite winced. "I wouldn't blame her for it, she is doing what she sees as best for the bigger picture, for the good of all. She didn't mean either of you any harm."

Greg could feel an unfamiliar emotion bubbling up within him. It was so rare for him to feel angry that it took a few moments for him to identify it.

"How dare she? Angel of Destiny or not, how dare she decide what is right for us? How dare anyone but us decide that?" He went to the lounge and picked up the phone. He was halfway through dialling Sarah's number when he felt a hand on his shoulder.

"She had no ill will toward either of you, honestly."

"I don't care! This isn't right!" Greg finished dialling the number, and waited impatiently for Sarah to answer, so he could tell the Angel of Destiny exactly what he thought of her bigger picture.

*   *   *

Despite his lack of enthusiasm, Jaron had managed to get Gold to attend the meeting arranged by Starlight, with all of the other earthbound Elders she could locate. There were seven of them there, all men, all of an advanced age, except for Gold, whose appearance was decades younger.

"We have all been called to meet today, by Sarah, also known as Starlight, the Angel of Destiny. She believes that if we work together we can guide this world into the Golden Age. I'm still a little hazy on the specifics on how this is meant to happen, as Sarah didn't go into detail. I think she hopes that we will gather, and our collective energy and wisdom will bring the necessary answers."

Gold was half-listening to Howard speak, but he was mostly focussed on trying to decide whether or not to stay. He was finding Earth to be cold, (even though it was apparently summer) and human life to be a struggle. He was so out of the habit of dealing with human necessities, such as eating and sleeping, that he was finding them to be a chore. He wished he'd stayed on the Other Side, with the Indigo Child, and waited for Starlight there.

"Gold, how do you feel about the situation? Having recently arrived on Earth, do you have any ideas of what it is we can do to take the world into the Golden Age? We have no previous experience of this, no way of knowing what might work."

Gold blinked at the sound of his name, and tried to focus on the question being asked of him. He cleared his throat. "Despite my connection with Starlight, I know as much as you do about this shift, this transition into the Golden Age. As you all know, we are on the second version of this timeline, and in the first one, the world ended in a way that had nothing to do with humans, so even if we do transition into the Golden Age, I have no reason to believe that the ending will be any different. I guess we will just have a slightly nicer life until it happens."

He took a few moments to register the frown and murmurs around the room. "I'm sorry, I know that we have come together to seek a positive future for the humans, but that is the reality as I see it."

The men were silent for a while. "You may have a point," Dominic said. "It's true that the world ended in the original timeline in a way that had nothing to do with human activity, and that we may well be headed for the same fate. But that is still a few years away yet. What we are concerned with, is if we can change the story of what happens before then."

"And because this is a second take, we can experiment a little. Everyone on Earth has already lived their life to the end of the world once. So if we change things, and their lives are different this time, hopefully better, then surely it's worth it?" Jaron asked.

Gold shrugged. He had lost interest in the discussion. He just wanted to be with Starlight. He was experiencing more and more human emotions and feelings, and at the moment he was feeling particularly self-involved. He couldn't understand why she couldn't see that it was the best thing for them. And for all the world. If they were together, he would feel inspired, and he would be able to happily experiment with the other Elders on how to improve the lives of humans.

He frowned. Was this a test? Was she pushing him away to see if he would fight for her? He knew that previously he had been quite passive in their relationship, and had kept his distance when told to, and had respectfully kept her wishes at all times.

But what if she really wanted him to just turn up on her doorstep and declare his love for her, and say that he wasn't going anywhere, or doing anything until they were together? And that he would do whatever it took to make it happen?

He stood up suddenly, stopping the conversation that had been happening around him. "I need to go." He looked at Jaron.

"I'll see you later, fill me in then, okay?"

Jaron nodded, looking a little confused.

Gold grabbed his jacket and left Howard's house. He paused outside for a moment to get his bearings. They had driven there in Jaron's car, but he had noticed a bus stop out on the street.

He strode down the driveway, and when he reached the street, he turned left and went to the bus stop. After studying the timetable and looking at the map, he figured that there would be a bus along in just a few minutes that would take him back to the village where Starlight lived. It was still school time. He could get there before she had to pick up the kids. He needed to tell her that he would do whatever it took for them to have a life together on Earth.

Or, at least for them to have these last few years together before the end.

The journey on the bus seemed to take an age, and Gold couldn't sit still in his seat. He jumped off at the nearest stop to Starlight's house, and after stopping at the corner shop for a bouquet of flowers, (a human custom he didn't entirely understand, but felt appropriate) he all but ran to Starlight's home.

Out of breath, he stood on the doorstep for a few moments before knocking on the door.

When she answered, Gold didn't even give her a chance to speak.

"I love you. I love you more than anything or anyone else in the Universe. I want to spend all my earthly moments with you before we go to the stars together. I don't see how there could be any possible reason why us being apart is for the good of all humanity or for us, and I will do whatever it takes to be with you."

Sarah smiled and motioned for him to enter the house. She took the flowers from him, and smelled them.

"These are beautiful, I'll put them in some water."

Gold followed her to the kitchen, frowning. Why wasn't she responding to his declaration?

He watched her unwrap the bouquet, trim the ends of the stalks, fill a vase with water, and then artistically arrange the flowers. Then she put the kettle on, got out two mugs and turned to him.

"Gold, you know that I love you too, more than anything in the Universe, but-"

Gold crossed the room in two strides and placed his lips against hers before she could finish her sentence. He kissed her softly at first, then when she responded, wrapping her arms around him, his kisses became more urgent. When they broke apart a few minutes later, they were both breathless.

Sarah released him and poured the hot water onto the tea bags, then added the milk and a sugar each.

Gold's hands were shaking as he took the mug from her. In all the time they had been together, nothing had prepared him for the intensity of emotion and feeling that had run through him in those moments of kissing her.

"Gold, I'm sorry," Sarah started.

"No, let me continue," Gold cut in. "For the world to shift into the Golden Age, we need as many Flames to reunite as possible, yes?"

Sarah nodded and sipped her tea.

"Then we need to show them it is indeed possible. If the Angel of Destiny and an Elder cannot figure out how to reunite, what hope does anyone else have of making it work?"

Gold watched Starlight's face, and could see a million emotions and thoughts flitting around in her mind. He could see that he had brought a new perspective she hadn't considered.

"Do you believe it is possible? For us to unite, to thrive in this Earthly realm, and to not be derailed from our missions?"

"I know it is possible," Gold said with absolute conviction. "I sat in the Elder meeting today, completely disinterested in the discussion, because all I could think about was how I didn't want to be on this planet unless I had you by my side. And that's when I realised that I needed to fight for you. That I need you by my side to be able to fulfil any kind of mission here on Earth."

Sarah sighed. "I had a phone call from Greg early this morning. He was very upset that I had been meddling with his union with Violet. He too believed that it should be possible for them to fulfil their missions while being together, that they are strong enough to do so. I think perhaps I have under-estimated them, and also myself, and you."

"Yes, you have. Velvet and Laguz, I mean, Violet and Greg also need to be together. They are so much stronger for it. When separated, their power and energy is diluted, faded. Their love is so vibrant, it could Awaken the world. Just as ours can."

Sarah smiled. "You may be right, but there are still practical things to consider," she said. "I have two kids, and a husband. I have responsibilities and obligations to fulfil."

"Would you rather be with your husband than with me?" Gold asked, only slightly afraid of the answer.

"No, of course not. I mean, I love him, but he is not my Flame." Sarah sighed. "Though not my Flame, he has been my rock on the Earth, providing for me and the children. I need time to be able to let him go, it won't just happen overnight."

Gold nodded. "I understand that, I don't expect you to just pack up and leave. Anyway, I need to make sure I have somewhere you can come to. I need to make sure I can provide for you and the children. And I am more than willing to do all of those things, if I know that is what you want, and that we will be united."

Sarah was silent for a while, and all Gold could hear was the ticking of the kitchen clock and the beat of his own heart.

"Yes," she said finally. "That is what I want. To have a human life with you is a dream I have held dearly in my heart and soul for aeons. I have just been afraid to try and make it work, in case it takes me away from my main purpose here."

"That is the difficulty that all Flames will face – the ability to pursue their mission while having a harmonious union. We must show them it is possible."

Sarah smiled and glanced up at the clock. "Yes, I agree, but right now, I need to go and pick up the kids. Let's meet again tomorrow, and make a plan. I need to make sure there is as little disruption to the kids as possible during this."

Gold nodded. "I will speak to Jaron on how I can create a home for us, and provide for us. He has many connections, and has been most helpful to me."

"That sounds like a good idea. I will come over tomorrow

at eleven."

Sarah moved toward Gold and they kissed again. This time, Gold felt a deep serenity wash over him. He couldn't wait to live a human life together with his Flame.

"I'll see you tomorrow," he whispered.

"Yes, you will," Sarah replied.

*   *   *

"Are we really making any difference at all here?"

Emerald smiled at Olivine. "Of course, why do you question it?"

"Because Gold and Starlight were not meant to reunite, but then Gold decided they would. And the same is happening to Greg and Violet, thanks to Aragonite's confession. So despite what we do here, they all still have the free will to rebel against what we are trying to direct them towards."

"But don't you see?" Mica said. "That's the beauty of it."

Olivine frowned. "I don't understand."

"Even though they may not follow the paths we are nudging them onto, by experiencing these new things, these new possibilities, they are in fact realising what they truly love, and what they truly want."

"If Starlight hadn't pushed Gold away, he may not have discovered the fire within him to fight?" Tektite asked.

"Yes, and if Greg hadn't lost Violet again, he might not have realised that it was actually possible for them to thrive together."

Labradorite winced. "Isn't it too late now? Violet has moved on. She and David spent the night together."

"I am confident that Greg and Violet will be able to move past that, if they both wish to. Of course, Violet has free will. If she chooses to return to Arizona to be with David, she could do that too."

Olivine sighed. "So we just keep doing what we're doing, and just adjust our course every now and then?"

"Yes, but we also must respect the decisions of those we are nudging. Now that Greg has decided that he wishes to be with Violet, then we mustn't try to nudge him away from that again."

"Why not?" Olivine asked. "We have not been very respectful of free will up until now."

Emerald glanced at Mica, uncertain of what to say. "I guess you could say that, though I see it as nudging them onto a path for their higher good, not disrespecting their free will. In a way, we are helping them to define and truly know what it is they want. It is time for souls on Earth to make definite decisions, to move forward with clarity, not just stumble along on a path they think might be the right one for them."

"I think I understand," Tektite said. "It just all seems like a big grey area."

"It is," Emerald agreed. "When Pearl went to Earth with her team to save lives, she wrestled with the same issues. Should she really be changing the fate of humans on Earth? Is it the right thing to do? Is it disregarding free will? But if she hadn't gone, if she hadn't saved the life of the child in hospital who was on the very brink of coming home, then we would not even be having this conversation. We would simply be sat at the lake, watching humans head for pretty much the same fate as they did in the original timeline."

"It wasn't a terrible fate," Labradorite commented.

"But it wasn't the happiest, brightest one," Emerald countered. "Imagine the beauty, the light that could be created and experienced in the next few years."

"So what is our next strategy? To reunite the Flames, even if they are married to other people as Starlight is? Won't that just create discord?" Olivine asked.

"I think that reuniting as many Flames as we can must be our mission, yes. Because the strength of their unconditional love is what the world needs right now. It may well break up marriages, but then we need to change the old relationship paradigms, and give people permission to seek out the deepest, most loving union they could possibly have."

"Let's do it," Labradorite said. "If Gold and Starlight can make it happen, and Greg and Violet can heal from their separation, and continue to run the retreats, then I don't see why other Flames shouldn't be able to make it work too."

"I think the number of Flames uniting at the Retreat is about to be magnified a million fold," Mica commented, looking around the room at the determined Angels.

Emerald smiled at her Flame.

"I think you're right."

Chapter Eighteen

Violet read the email from her best friend, tears streaming down her face. She didn't even care that she was sat in a busy café in Santa Monica.

Amy's mother had passed away really suddenly, after being diagnosed with an aggressive form of cancer. Amy had been with her at the time, but although she knew that her mother was with the Angels now, she was absolutely heartbroken.

Violet dug around in her bag for a tissue, and blew her nose. She felt awful that instead of being with her friend in her time of need, she was halfway around the world, having a great time. She was so glad that Amy had Joe, and hoped he was taking good care of her friend.

She wrote an email back, asking when the funeral would be, and if there was anything she could do. She hoped that the funeral wouldn't be until the following week, when she would be home. She felt the same blanket of sadness settle across her shoulders, as when she had hugged her friend months before at the Spiritual Sisters meeting. She sighed. It had been a premonition of this very moment.

Violet sent the email, then smiled when a message from David popped up. He had sent one every day since she'd left Arizona, and his words always made her smile.

She replied with a picture she'd taken earlier of Venice

Beach, and then set her phone down and sipped her drink.

Despite all that had happened, she still thought of Greg in every moment. She twisted her ring around her finger, and remembered the day of her wedding, of walking down the grassy aisle to where Greg stood at the end. In the moment she had said her vows, she never would have imagined in a million years that she would be considering the proposal of another man. Not that David had asked her to marry him, but asking her to relocate to another continent to be with him was a pretty big proposal.

But why was she even considering it? Based on the reading of a crazed crystal ball reader in New York? Based on her own weird feelings? And on Greg pushing her away? What was it that was making her think that it would be a good idea?

While musing over this, her phone vibrated. When she saw the name on the message, her eyes widened. Despite the physical distance, it seemed that Greg was still able to hear her thoughts.

She clicked on the message, and as she read, her eyes grew wider still.

"Violet, I know that we said we would not contact each other unless it was an emergency, but I believe that in a way, this is an emergency. I have recently been informed that Starlight has gathered a team of Angels in the Angelic Realm who are basically tasked with nudging people on Earth toward paths that would create the best bigger picture for the planet. They are messing with our free will, and apparently our separation was orchestrated by them. Since finding out, my feelings of unease and uncertainty over our relationship have vanished, and after some sessions with Lisa to clear the past, I feel that I have healed our past issues too. With a clear heart and mind, I have found that I love you, absolutely, unconditionally and unequivocally, and when you are finished with your trip, I would love nothing more than for you to come home, and be with me. I miss you, Violet. But if things have changed for you, then I understand. After all, I said we should both be free to do as we wished. Please contact me when you get this, love for eternity, Greg."

The tears really were flowing now, and Violet found herself

getting filled with anger as well as with love.

How could Sarah do that to her? How could she mess with her relationship with Greg? When she knew how important he was to her? How much she loved him?

Did that mean that her feelings for David weren't real? That they had been planted? Manufactured?

The idea of the manipulation of her emotions and feelings made her feel even more angry, and without thinking of the cost or the time difference, she picked up her phone and dialled Sarah's number.

"Hello?" The groggy voice of her friend made her check the time. It would be three in the morning in the UK.

"Sarah?"

"Violet? Is that you? What's wrong? Are you okay?"

"No, I'm not okay! Greg just sent me a message. Is it true? Have you been manipulating us? Did you separate us?"

She heard Sarah sigh, and then she could hear shuffling noises as she got out of bed and moved to another room.

"As I explained to Greg, it was all to ensure that the world would move into the Golden Age. I asked an Angel to build a team to make the necessary nudges, and they decided that your separation from Greg would be necessary."

"What about me meeting someone else? The psychic in New York? Was that set up?"

"I don't know, Violet, like I said, the Angels in the Angelic Realm know the specifics, but I don't. Have you met someone else?"

Violet was quiet for a while. She felt betrayed by her friend, and was unsure as to whether she still trusted her. But she also needed some advice.

"Yes. I met someone. And he has asked me to move to America to be with him."

"Oh, wow," Sarah said. "What have you said?"

"That I would think about it. I genuinely felt a connection to him, and it seemed like the right thing to do, but now I'm all confused. Because what if the connection isn't real? What if it's just the creation of a bunch of Angels who think they know what's best?"

Sarah sighed again. "Oh, Violet, I'm sorry, I really am. I knew there would be issues with this whole thing, and I swear I would never have created the team and given them universal permission to do what they are doing if I didn't think it would work, and take the world into the Golden Age. But I can understand your anger and frustration. All I can suggest is that you really go into your heart, your soul, and listen only to your inner voice. Ignore the psychic, ignore any outside whispering. Go within. You know the truth, you know who you really love and where you really want to be."

Violet nodded, her anger lessening. "Thank you. You're right. I guess I have been following the signs quite blindly, trusting that if it all happened this easily, then it must be the right thing to do, but perhaps it all happened a bit too easily to be the right thing for me."

"How does Greg feel?"

"He loves me, and wants me to come home. But then he doesn't know about David."

"Ah," Sarah said. "I'm sorry, Violet. I hope that whatever you decide, Greg understands."

Tears fell again. "I hope so too," Violet said, sniffing.

"Are we okay, Sister?" Sarah asked softly.

Violet was silent for a few moments. She was still hurt, but her anger had subsided. "Yes, we're okay. But please, don't ever do anything like that again, okay?"

"I won't. I promise."

"Okay then. I better go, this is probably costing a fortune, and you should go back to sleep, I'm sorry I woke you."

"It's okay. I love you, Violet."

"Love you too, Sarah. Good night."

Violet hung up the phone and opened Greg's email again. She read the words over and over until they were blurred with her tears. She had no idea how to reply. Would he really be able to forgive her? She knew she would have to tell him, he would be able to tell she was hiding something otherwise.

She closed her eyes and went deep within, and asked herself, did she really want to be with David? Or did she want to return to Greg?

After a few moments, the answer came to her. She opened her eyes and smiled.

*   *   *

"You look tired, my love."

Sarah smiled wearily at Gold. "Violet called me last night, Greg had contacted her, and she was upset."

Gold frowned. "You never really explained what you meant by the meddling? How did you interfere with their relationship?"

Sarah sighed, and then as briefly as she could, explained what had been going on right underneath his nose in the Angelic Realm without his knowledge.

"So the rumours were true? Pearl lied to me? An Angelic Rebellion! Emerald and Mica are running it now? And Aragonite is here? Does Pallas know?"

"Yes, the rumours were true. Pallas doesn't know, Emerald and Mica are running it, and Aragonite is here." Sarah smiled. "But I sent a message, after speaking with Violet last night, for them to pull back a little, and to allow the souls they have been nudging to make their own decisions, and to only nudge them to listen to their own hearts."

"Starlight, I am shocked," Gold said, a heavy feeling of disappointment settling within. "Humans on Earth are not puppets, we cannot make them do things they do not wish to do, it's not right."

Sarah nodded. "I know, and I may have been wrong doing what I did, but it worked on the rogue planets! Just enough nudges to the right people meant that the whole world – the whole of their civilisation – was nudged toward a more harmonious future. And I felt that the free will of a few was a small enough sacrifice for the wellbeing of the majority. Besides, you sent Pearl and her team to Earth to meddle with free will and destiny. And it worked, didn't it?"

"That was different," Gold protested.

"Was it?" Sarah asked softly.

Gold was quiet for a while, he stared into the fire in the

hearth, and tried to work out how he felt. There was a part of him that was disgusted by her behaviour, but there was another part that was... jealous? He frowned as he examined this feeling. He realised that for centuries he had been blamed for doing exactly as Starlight had been doing, and yet, he had not been doing that at all. But he had wanted to. Goodness had he wanted to. A nudge there, a push here. He could have vastly improved the lives of many, so many times. But he had resisted, all in the name of free will.

How could he blame Starlight for doing this, especially when she was doing it to improve the lives of the entire human race, and not for any egoic purposes?

"Are you angry?" Sarah said softly. "I wouldn't blame you if you were. I seem to have hurt many people in my mission to help."

Gold sighed. "No, I am not angry, I do understand why you acted as you did, and why I was not informed. I would have likely shut it down had I known while still on the Other Side."

Sarah smiled. "Yes, I saw that possibility."

"I must ask though, has the bigger picture really changed that dramatically as a result of the Angelic intervention?"

"Yes, it has. In fact, I am certain now that we will experience the Golden Age in this lifetime."

Gold was shocked into silence. "Absolutely certain?" he whispered.

"Yes," Sarah said, reaching out to touch his hand. "And you know what tipped it?"

Gold shook his head. He honestly had no idea.

"You."

"Me?" he asked, frowning. "I didn't do anything."

"Yes, you did." Sarah stood up and pulled him to his feet also. She pulled him closer, and he breathed in her scent.

"You came here. And then you fought for me, you fought for our love. And in that moment, you changed the world."

Chapter Nineteen

Greg waited nervously in the Arrivals area at Gatwick, holding a handmade sign with Violet's name on it, and a bouquet of purple roses. The only response he'd had to his message was her flight number and the time she would be landing. So he had no idea what she had decided, whether she wanted to be with him or not.

He sensed there was something big that she wanted to tell him, and every time he wondered what it was, his heart skipped a beat. He hoped that he could deal with whatever it was. He knew that she had been influenced by the Angels, and that whatever had happened in America wouldn't have been entirely her own decision, which would hopefully make it easier to accept.

A crowd of people came through the doors from the baggage reclaim area, and Greg scanned their faces. When he saw a familiar purple scarf, he grinned and waved his sign at his Flame. She spotted him and smiled tiredly. She headed straight toward him but instead of greeting him with a hug or kiss as he'd expected, she stopped a foot away from him.

"Hi," she said.

"Hi," he replied. His heart was now thudding in his chest, and in an effort to gloss over the awkward moment, he reached out to take her case from her and motioned for her to follow him. She took the flowers and sign from him and smiled.

"I've always dreamed of being greeted at the airport by someone holding a sign with my name on it," she said.

"Your wish is my command," Greg joked as they left the airport and went out to the multi-storey car park. Greg paid for the parking ticket and then led her back to the van. They had still not touched and Greg was getting worried.

What was the big thing she was not telling him?

He loaded her case into the back of the van, then joined her in the front. Violet was silent while he navigated his way out of the airport and onto the main road, heading home.

He couldn't bear the thought of a silent, three hour journey, or fake small talk, so he decided to get straight to the point.

"What is it, Violet? Please tell me."

Violet sighed, and he saw her staring down at her lap out of the corner of his eye. "I should know you can read me like a book," she said.

"You know you can tell me anything. I just need to know."

"Okay, well, I met someone."

Although he was prepared for her to say something like that, it still felt like a punch in the gut. "Tell me about him."

"He came to an event in Arizona, and then asked me to dinner after the event. I was tired but hungry, so I said yes. We got on really well, and he offered me rides to the next three events. On my last night in Arizona, we went out for dinner again, and he basically asked me to live in Arizona with him."

Greg stamped a bit too hard on the brakes, making them both jolt forward against their seatbelts. "Sorry," he muttered. "Carry on."

"I left for LA, and he said to think about it. And that if I wanted to be with him, I could just fly back to Arizona from LA and stay there until my visa ran out, then after that, we would figure things out."

Greg began to breathe a little easier. "But you came home instead?"

"Amy's mum's funeral is next week, I needed to come home to be with her. Her mum had been so good to me, I couldn't miss it. I feel bad enough that I didn't see her before she went."

"And after the funeral?" Greg struggled to get the words

out. "Are you going back to him?

There was a long pause, and it took all of Greg's concentration to keep the van on the road.

"No. I'm not. I did feel a connection to him, and I really liked him, but after you told me about the Angelic intervention, I realised that despite my attraction to him, there really was something not quite right. So I realised that the attraction might well have been manufactured."

Greg nodded. "So did you tell him? That you weren't going back?"

"Yes, he was fine about it. He wanted to stay friends, which I thought might be too weird at first, but I think it could work."

"Why would it be weird?" Greg asked, hoping that the answer wasn't what he suspected.

"Because, well, because we kissed. And also..." Violet's voice trailed off, and Greg's heart stopped.

"Also?"

"I stayed the night at his place."

Greg swallowed hard and gripped the steering wheel a little too tightly. He'd never considered himself to be a jealous person before, but it felt like there was a monster raging inside him. "Did you...?"

"No. We didn't. But we did sleep in the same bed."

Greg exhaled loudly and Violet glanced at him.

"I'm sorry. I know you don't really want to hear this," Violet said.

"No, I do. And besides. I was the one who said we should be free to do as we wanted, even see other people. I can't be angry with you for doing what I suggested. I guess I just wasn't prepared for it becoming a reality."

"Did you... see anyone else?"

Greg heard the fear in her voice and smiled. "No, I didn't. Although..." He heard a sharp intake of breath and he wondered if he should continue. He didn't want to hurt her, but then he also didn't want to keep any secrets from her either. "Lisa and I kissed. She was upset about Missy dying, and she had been remembering our life in Atlantis, and it just lasted a moment. But then we both realised how wrong it felt. I think maybe we had both been nudged too." He waited for her response, wondering if she would be able to forgive him, and her close friend.

"She messaged me about Missy, it seems that a few souls went home while I was away." Violet sighed. "Do you feel anything for Lisa?"

Greg shook his head. "We're just friends. I was really just a shoulder to cry on, she was missing her Flame, feeling lonely, and then grieving. That's all it was. And I was missing you, too."

"I missed you too," Violet said.

Greg glanced at her and could see her tears shining in the headlights of the cars passing them. He reached over to squeeze her knee, in the same way he did so often when they travelled all over Europe together.

"Were you really worried how I would take your news?" he asked gently.

Violet wiped her eyes with her hand and nodded. "Yes. I wasn't sure you'd want to kiss me, or touch me. And I wouldn't have blamed you."

"Oh, Violet. I love you. So much. And I don't blame you for what happened, even if it was real attraction and not just the Angels meddling, you were doing what you needed to move on, to move forward. I only hope you can forgive me and Lisa too."

"I just felt so terrible that I was cheating on you." Violet was crying quietly now, and Greg felt helpless to comfort her. He watched her for a few moments, then when he turned his attention back to the road, he swore loudly, making Violet look up.

He slammed the brakes on, but he couldn't tell in the darkness if he had acted soon enough. The traffic was at a standstill on the motorway in front of them, and he hadn't noticed.

"Greg!" Violet cried out.

He kept pumping the brake pedal, but they had been doing a reasonable speed, and the large vehicle had a lot of momentum behind it. Everything went into slow motion, and Greg managed to check if the hard shoulder was empty.

It was.

Praying silently he wrenched the steering wheel to the side and pulled over onto the hard shoulder. They came to a stop, and Greg closed his eyes. Had he not pulled over, he would definitely have ploughed into the cars in front.

"Are you okay?" he asked Violet, who was shaking a little.

She nodded. "Yes, I'm okay. Thank goodness you thought to pull over, I would have frozen."

Greg undid his seatbelt and reached over to hug Violet. "I'm so sorry."

"It's okay, we're okay, the campervan is okay. The Angels were looking after us. But maybe we should save the serious talks for when we're not in a moving vehicle!"

Greg chuckled and pulled back. "Yes, I think that's probably wise."

"So *are* we okay then?" Violet asked quietly.

"Yes," Greg replied firmly. "Neither of us did anything wrong. I love you, and nothing will ever change that."

Violet smiled at her Flame. "I love you too. For eternity."

"For eternity."

*   *   *

"Oh, thank the goddess," Emerald muttered as she watched Violet and Greg return to the Retreat, and embrace one another. She couldn't believe that they'd worked things out, only to nearly die in a car accident. It had taken a big nudge to make Greg pull over when he did. She was surprised that nothing more had happened between Violet and David, but she was glad it hadn't. And the news of Greg kissing Lisa had been a surprise, she wondered how she had missed that development.

The only thing she felt bad about now was raising David's hopes of a harmonious relationship, only to dash them again.

"I know, I feel bad about Bk too. I mean, David," Mica said, without looking up from his own basin. "I've been looking, and I think I might have found his Flame."

"Bk's Flame? Is she on Earth?"

"I think so, but she lives in Scotland. I'm going to put a nudge in to help their paths to cross."

"Do you think that's a good idea? We're not meant to be meddling as much. Don't you think he needs to do some inner work first? Heal from his wife cheating on him, then Violet turning him down?"

Mica looked up. "Actually, he has been doing the inner work. He has been reading a lot on letting go, and he has seen a healer at the same store where he met Violet. It will take a little while for him to meet his Twin, and I think by the time they do meet, he will be ready, as will she. I'm simply guiding them to listen to their hearts."

Emerald smiled. "Then by all means, nudge away. I would love to see him happy, he's such a lovely soul, and as always so helpful at the Academy. Do you think Violet will realise at some point who David was?"

Mica shrugged. "Maybe. They were going to keep in touch, so perhaps they'll work it out one day. It's not really important, though it might help them to understand why they had such a strong connection to one another."

"Indeed."

"Emerald? Mica?"

The two Angels looked up to see Tektite with an Angel who was not on the Angelic Intervention Team.

"Yes, Tektite?" Emerald asked.

"This is Ammonite. She would like to join the AIT."

Emerald stood to greet the Angel. "Welcome, Ammonite, may I ask why you would like to join the team?"

Ammonite nodded. "I have recently just returned home from Earth, and I heard that you were working more closely with those there to make the Golden Age happen, and that you were specifically working with Velvet, Laguz and their close friends, as you believe that they will have a significant impact."

"Yes, that is all true," Emerald said, wondering if Galena would ever stop spreading the word of their secret operation.

"I was the mother of a close friend of Velvet's," Ammonite continued.

"You were Amy's mother? Athena's?"

Ammonite nodded. "Yes I was blessed with the task of raising my beautiful Angel daughter, whose power and standing in the Angelic Realm I am only just realising and remembering now. I wish to keep a close eye on her, and help her at any point that I can to have a joyous and love-filled life. I know she is devastated that I left so suddenly, and I need her to know that I am still here."

Emerald nodded. "I completely understand. Please, join our team, and do that. We have been asked by Starlight to take change tacks slightly with our nudging, and while we work out our new roles, it may be a little quiet for a while."

Ammonite nodded. "That's perfect. I don't want to watch my daughter constantly. I just want to make sure I can connect with her when she needs me most."

"And you shall, Angel. Tektite will show you around and tell you all you need to know."

Tektite nodded and led Ammonite away, and Emerald sat back down.

"Amy would be so pleased to know her mother is here with us, and is helping her," Mica said.

"Yes, it's a shame we can't just talk to her directly, and tell her what is going on."

"I think she knows, deep in her heart."

"I hope so."

* * *

When Violet woke up in Greg's arms, snug and safe in his embrace, she knew unequivocally that she had made the right decision. She thought back to when she awoke in David's bed, and how awful she'd felt when she realised how close she'd come to giving herself to a man she did not love. She realised now that it would be better to be alone than to be with someone whom she didn't love with every molecule of her heart and soul.

"Morning," Greg said sleepily.

Violet turned in his arms to face him, and kiss him gently. "Morning."

"Did you sleep okay?"

"Yes, I slept very well, considering how jet lagged I felt.

Shall I go and get us some breakfast?"

Greg shook his head. "No, I will go and make it. You stay here, I won't be long."

Violet kissed him again, and then allowed him to release her and get up, stretching as he went. He threw on a t-shirt and underpants, then went downstairs.

Violet reached over to the bedside table to pick up her phone. There were messages from all her friends asking if she got home okay. She replied to them all, writing a longer message to Amy to see if she was okay, and if she needed any help with the funeral arrangements.

There was also a message from David.

She smiled as she read his words, and hoped that he would find his own Flame one day. He truly was a wonderful man who deserved to be loved unconditionally.

She replied to his message to let him know she had arrived safely, and that she and Greg were back together, and all was good. She added that if he ever wanted to attend the Twin Flame Retreat, then he was welcome to any time, as her guest.

She frowned, wondering how Greg would feel about it, but then shrugged. The likelihood of him ever attending was slim, so there was no point worrying about it. It seemed like a nice gesture to make though.

A little while later, Greg reappeared with a tray filled with food and drink. Violet sat up in bed and Greg joined her. They ate and talked, and Violet enjoyed the lazy morning. It wasn't often they took things easy, but one of the things they had decided on was that they needed to take more time off, to spend time relaxing together, but also to have their own time to themselves too. They couldn't keep going relentlessly, or they'd burn out like Esmeralda had.

"Let's take the camper away for the weekend in October," Violet said. "I've been wanting to go to the Lake District for ages, and it would be nice to go there before it gets really cold, to see the autumn colours."

Greg nodded. "That sounds really nice, I like that idea. I'm sure we can make it happen."

Violet smiled and reached out to wipe the jam from corner

of his mouth. "Good, then in the new year we can plan some other short breaks too. There is so much of this country I still haven't seen, it's criminal really."

"It might not be as exciting as touring the US, but I'm sure it would be fun to explore new places here."

"The trip was really good, and I'm glad I did it, I met some wonderful Earth Angels who were so ready to read the book, and to remember who they really were. And I met more souls from the Academy! In Canada, I met Chiffon, the Professor of Manifestation! How mad is that?"

"I don't find it in the least bit mad," Greg said with a smile as he finished his toast. "I think it's perfectly normal now."

Violet giggled. "True, I guess it is quite 'normal'," she said, making quote mark gestures with her fingers. "We've gone beyond things seeming weird."

"Definitely. Wouldn't know what normal was if it bit me, to be honest."

Violet's phone buzzed and she picked it up to see a message from Sarah. It was a brief one, saying she would see her at the funeral, and that she had some big news. Violet frowned, wondering what the news would be.

"Is Amy okay?" Greg asked.

Violet sighed. "She's not great, but that's to be expected. I'll speak to her later. That was a message from Sarah, she has big news."

Greg raised his eyebrows. "Has she decided to stop meddling in people's love lives?"

Violet chuckled. "Let's hope so. Are you still mad at her? She said you gave her quite the telling off."

Greg shrugged. "Mostly. I mean, it's worked out okay between us, but if things hadn't worked out, I don't know, perhaps I would have held a grudge."

"You know that she had the best of intentions really," Violet said, even though she had been really angry too.

"Yeah, I know." Greg shrugged. "Still not right though."

"So what did I miss? I know I said not to send updates, but it feels strange not knowing what's been happening here."

"Oh! Yeah, there were some pretty big developments," Greg

said, reaching over to his bedside table. He handed a piece of paper to Violet.

She took it and scanned the text. It was the article about the dream recorder. "Oh, yeah, I knew about this, I meant to tell you about it."

"You knew? How did you find out?"

Violet smiled wryly. "The David in the article is the David I met in Arizona."

Greg's eyebrows shot up. "You kissed the inventor of the dream recorder? Did you get to try it?"

Violet chuckled, then frowned. "No, actually I didn't. I didn't think to ask! How silly of me. But it means it worked, doesn't it? Our manifestation ritual?"

"Yes, that's what we decided, so we had another circle to see what else we could manifest, and we took it in turns to say what we wanted."

"You did?" Violet asked, trying not to feel unneeded or left out. "And did that work too?" She kind of hoped he would say no.

"Yes, it did, Julie said she wanted a relationship with her soulmate, and about five minutes later, Aragonite knocked on the front door!"

Violet's hand flew to her mouth and she gasped. "Her Twin Flame? The Angel who went to another galaxy? He's here? But how?"

Greg smiled. "I'll let Julie and Aragonite tell you the story, they're away with the kids this weekend, but they'll be back in a couple of days."

Violet shook her head. "That's really amazing." She frowned. "What did you ask for?"

Greg looked a bit sheepish. "Oh, um, help with my heating system."

Violet laughed loudly, and he grinned. "I should have known," she said. "Did that work too?"

"Not instantly, but a couple of days ago I had a breakthrough with my design. I might even be able to sell the concept too, and make some money from it as well."

Violet reached over to kiss him. "I'm glad."

"What would you have asked for, if you'd been there?"

Violet sat back and thought about it. But she couldn't think of anything she actually needed or wanted than what she had right in that moment. Her thoughts flitted back to her trip around America.

"I wouldn't ask for anything for myself. But I would ask for my friend Saphron to find her Flame, for David to find his Flame, and for Robert to be healed, healthy and well again."

Greg smiled. "Why are you so good? You could have asked for a better car or a new wardrobe or even a film deal for your book. But instead you ask for things for your friends."

Violet shrugged. "I'm happy right now, and I just want everyone else to be happy, too."

Greg leaned forward and kissed her slowly. "I'm very happy right now too," he whispered.

Violet smiled. "There is one more thing I need to tell you."

Greg raised an eyebrow. "Sounds serious?"

Violet sighed. "The main reason I gave David a chance, and really considered being with him, and not you, was because of a reading I had in New York."

"A reading?"

"Yes, I had a reading in this tiny little place with the strangest guy. It was really accurate. He told me things that I haven't ever told anyone." She looked down at her hands, remembering the man tracing the lines on her skin. "Then he told me about Rose."

"Rose? Who's that?" Greg asked.

"My daughter. The one I would have had if I were to be with a man called David."

Greg was silent for a while. "Oh, I see," he said finally. "He didn't see us with a child?"

Violet shook her head. "I didn't ask. He didn't give me much of a chance to speak. He just gave me the reading, asked for payment, then went silent." Violet tried to smile. "Like I said, he was very strange."

"But you believed him?"

"Not at first, but then…"

"Then you met David. In Arizona. A week later?"

"A few days, yes." Violet sighed. "It was a bit surreal at first, I was in shock that what the reader had said might come true. But when I met David, and I felt that connection with him, I could see the possibility of us being together, and having a child."

Greg sighed too. "Do you want to be with him? Because if you do, if you want the chance of having your daughter, I won't stand in your way."

Violet grabbed Greg's hand and gripped it tightly. "If I can't have a child with you, then I am not meant to have one. Nor do I want one if it is not yours." She touched Greg's face. "You're the one I want to be with. The one I am meant to be with." She shook her head. "David and I had a connection, but there was something..."

"Missing?" Greg filled in.

"Yes, missing. And I cannot live a lie just to have a child." Greg leaned over to kiss her, and the feeling of being home settled over her shoulders like a warm blanket.

"There it is," Violet whispered.

"There what is?" Greg asked.

"That feeling. That's what was missing."

"Home?" Greg whispered.

"Yes," Violet replied. "Home."

Chapter Twenty

Gold gripped Sarah's hand tightly, as they entered the church. He found it difficult to be in places such as these, with so many depictions of the misery he remembered so well.

"You're okay," Sarah whispered as they walked up the aisle to sit near the front.

Gold looked around and saw some familiar faces approaching.

"Sarah!"

Sarah let go of his hand to embrace Violet, and he immediately missed the warmth. When she pulled away from her friend, she reached out for him again.

"Violet, I want you to meet someone," Sarah said.

Violet's gaze met his, and he was surprised at how much she looked like her younger self in Atlantis. Violet frowned a little, and then stepped closer. His nervousness got the better of him, and his right eye began to visibly twitch.

Violet gasped and her hand flew to her mouth.

"Gold?" she whispered.

He nodded. "Hello, Velvet."

Eyes wide, Violet looked at Sarah, who nodded. "He came to be with me," she said simply.

Violet looked back at him, then she threw her arms around him, surprising him with a strong, coconut scented hug.

"It's so amazing to see you! I never thought I would live to see the day you returned to Earth. This really is big news!"

Gold released her and smiled. "It's very good to see you too."

Violet studied his face and shook her head. "You look so young! I would never have guessed it was you if you had been here alone."

"Gold, good to see you again," Greg said, reaching out to shake his hand.

"Likewise, Laguz. I'm pleased you are both also reunited."

"Yes, me too."

They looked up when they heard music begin to play. Gold and Starlight went to sit down, and Greg and Violet headed to the front where Amy sat, quietly weeping into a handkerchief.

*   *   *

Violet sat next to her best friend and gripped her hand tightly. Greg sat on her other side, and he squeezed Violet's knee reassuringly.

Amy leaned on her shoulder, and Violet looked up to see the vicar motioning for people to be seated before she took her place at the altar to begin the service. She looked at the beautiful white casket, and silently asked the Angels to send a sign that Amy's mother was okay, and was happily at home with them in the Angelic Realm.

When the organ started playing, and they rose to sing Amy's mother's favourite hymn, she heard Amy gasp next to her. She looked to see her friend hold her hand out, and out of nowhere, a perfectly formed white feather drifted down and landed in her palm.

Amy looked at Violet and smiled. "She's okay," she whispered.

Violet nodded and silently thanked the Angels.

"Yes, she is."

*   *   *

"That was perfect," Emerald said to Ammonite as they watched her funeral. "Amy knows you are with her now."

Ammonite smiled through her tears. "I really was ready to come home, but my heart aches for my girl. I wish I could have seen her get married, and have children. But the pull to be here again was so strong."

"You will see it all from here, you won't miss any of it. And Amy will know that you are with her every step of the way."

"I hope so."

"I know so," Emerald said with a smile. "Now, will I see you at the viewing? Please tell everyone you see. I'm trying to gather the troops."

Ammonite nodded. "Yes, I'll be there."

Emerald nodded and went to tell the Angels to all meet in the viewing room. She and Mica had discussed it, and they both felt it was time to use the last drop, and see the culmination of their efforts, and hopefully see the world moving into the Golden Age for themselves.

Not long later, she stood at the front of the room, the screen of mist swirling, and the Angels all watching expectantly. She dropped the last indigo drop into the mist, then stepped back to watch.

When the new destiny of the world had finished unfolding before her, Emerald smiled.

About the Author

Michelle lives in the UK, when she's not flitting in and out of other realms. She believes in Faeries and Unicorns and thinks the world needs more magic and fun in it. She writes because she would go crazy if she didn't. She might already be a little crazy, so please buy more books so she can keep writing.

Please feel free to write a review of this book. Michelle loves to get direct feedback, so if you would like to contact her, please e-mail theamethystangel@hotmail.co.uk or keep up to date by following her blog – **TwinFlameBlog.com.** You can also follow her on Twitter **@themiraclemuse** or like her page on Facebook.

You can now become an Earth Angel Trainee:
earthangelacademy.co.uk

To sign up to her mailing list, visit:
michellegordon.co.uk

Earth Angel Series:

The Earth Angel Training Academy (book 1)
There are humans on Earth, who are not, in fact, human.
They are **Earth Angels**.
Earth Angels are beings who have come from other realms,
dimensions and planets, and are choosing to be born on Earth in
human form for just **one** reason.
To **Awaken the world**.
Before they can carry out their perilous mission, they must first
learn how to be human.
The best place they can do that, is at
The Earth Angel Training Academy

The Earth Angel Awakening (book 2)
After learning how to be human at the Earth Angel Training
Academy, the Angels, Faeries, Merpeople and Starpeople are
born into human bodies on Earth.
Their Mission? **Awaken the world**.
But even though they **chose** to go to Earth, and they chose to be
human, it doesn't mean that it will be **easy** for them to Awaken
themselves.
Only if they **reconnect** to their **origins**,
and to other Earth Angels, will they will be able to **remember**
who they really are.
Only then, will they experience
The Earth Angel Awakening

The Other Side (book 3)

There is an Angel who holds the world in her hands.

She is the **Angel of Destiny**.

Her actions will start the **ripples** that will **save humans** from their certain demise.

In order for her to initiate the necessary changes, she must travel to other **galaxies**, and call upon the most **enlightened** and **evolved** beings of the Universe.

To save **humankind**.

When they agree, she wishes to prepare them for Earth life, and so invites them to attend the Earth Angel Training Academy, on

The Other Side

The Twin Flame Reunion (book 4)

The Earth Angels' missions are clear: **Awaken** the world, and move humanity into the **Golden Age**.

But there is another reason many of the Earth Angels choose to come to Earth.

To **reunite** with their **Twin Flames**.

The Twin Flame connection is deep, everlasting and intense, and happens only at the **end of an age**. Many Flames have not been together for millennia, some have never met.

Once on Earth, every Earth Angel longs to meet their Flame. The one who will make them **feel at home**, who will make living on this planet bearable.

But no one knows if they will actually get to experience

The Twin Flame Reunion

The Twin Flame Retreat (book 5)
The question in the minds of many Earth Angels
on Earth right now is:
Where is my **Twin Flame?**
Though many Earth Angels are now meeting their Flames, the
circumstances around their reunion can have
life-altering consequences.
If meeting your Flame meant your life would never be the same
again, would you still want to find them?
When in need of **support** and answers,
Earth Angels attend
The Twin Flame Retreat

The Twin Flame Resurrection (book 6)
Twin Flames are **destined** to meet. And when they are meant to
be together, nothing can keep them apart.
Not even **death**.
When Earth Angels go home to the Fifth Dimension too soon,
they have the **choice** to come back.
To be with their **Twin Flame**.
The connection can be so overwhelming, that some Earth Angels
try to resist it, try to push it away.
But it is **undeniable**.
When things don't go according to plan, the universe steps in,
and the Earth Angels experience
The Twin Flame Ressurrection

The Twin Flame Reality *(book 7)*

Being an Earth Angel on Earth can be difficult, especially when it doesn't feel like home, and when there's a deep longing for a realm or dimension where you feel you **belong**.

Finding a Twin Flame, is like **coming home**.

Losing one, can be **devastating**.

Adrift, lonely, isolated... an Earth Angel would be forgiven for preferring to go home, than to stay here
without their Flame.

But if they can find the **strength** to stay, to follow their mission to **Awaken** the world, and fulfil their original purpose, they will find they can be **happy** here.

Even despite the sadness of
The Twin Flame Reality

The Twin Flame Rebellion *(book 8)*

The Angels on the Other Side have a **duty** to **help** their human charges, but **only** when they are **asked** for help.

They are not allowed to meddle with **Free Will**.

But a number of Angels are asked to break their
Golden Rule, and start influencing the human
lives of the Earth Angels.

Once the Angels start nudging, they find they can't stop, and when the Earth Angels find out they are being manipulated from the Other Side, they aren't happy.

Determined to **choose** their own **fate**,
the Earth Angels embark on
The Twin Flame Rebellion

Visionary Collection:

Heaven dot com

When Christina goes into hospital for the final time, and knows that she is about to lose her battle with cancer, she asks her boyfriend, James, to help her deliver messages to her family and friends after she has gone.

She also asks him to do something for her, but she dies before he can make it happen, and he finds it difficult to forgive himself.

After her death, her messages are received by her loved ones, and the impact her words have will change their lives forever.

The Doorway to PAM

Natalie is an ordinary girl who has lost her way. There is nothing particularly special about her or her life. She has no exceptional abilities. She hasn't achieved anything miraculous. Her life has very little meaning to it.

Evelyn is the caretaker at Pam's. The alternate dimension where souls at their lowest point find the answers they need to turn their lives around. The dimension dreamers visit, to help people while they sleep.

One ordinary girl, one extraordinary woman.
One fated meeting that will change lives.

The Elphite

Ellie's life is just one long, bad case of déjà vu. She has lived her life before - a hundred times before - and she remembers each and every lifetime.

Each time, she has changed things, but has never managed to change the ending.

This time, in this life, she hopes that it will be different. So she makes the biggest change of all - she tries to avoid meeting him.

Her soulmate. The love of her life.

Because maybe if they don't meet, she can finally change her destiny.

But fate has other ideas...

I'm Here

When Marielle finds out that a guy she had a crush on in school has passed away, the strange occurrences of the previous week begin to make sense. She suspects that he is trying to give her a message from the other side, and so opens up to communicate with him, She has no idea that by doing so, she will be forming a bond so strong, that life as she knows it will forever be changed.

Nathan assumed that when he died, he would move on, and continue his spiritual journey. But instead he finds himself drawn to a girl that he once knew. The more he watches her, and gets to know her, he realises that he was drawn to her for a reason, and that once he knows what that is, he will be able to change his destiny.

designs from a
different planet

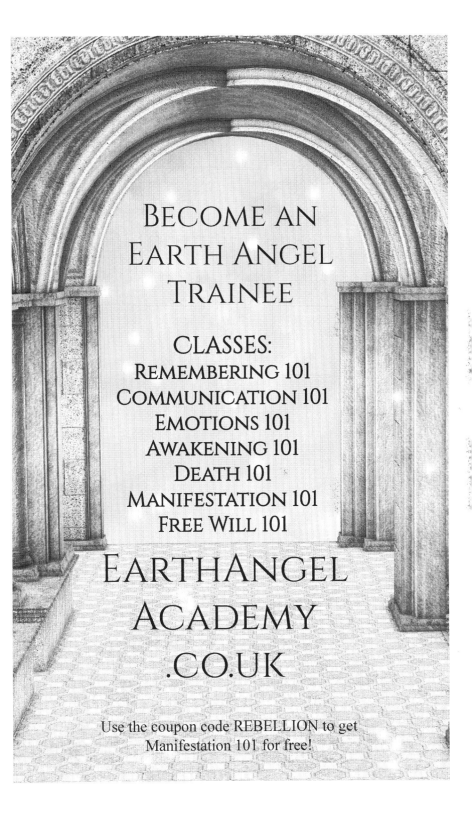

Earth Angel Sanctuary

Founded by Sarah Rebecca Vine in 2014, the Earth Angel Sanctuary has over 200 videos and audios (and growing), live calls every month and a Facebook family of like-minded souls.

With libraries including How-To Tutorials, an Energy and Vow Clearing Library, Rituals, Meditations, Activations and Bonuses, the Earth Angel Sanctuary has everything for those who have just discovered they are an earth angel to those who have been on their journey for a while and would love the additional love, support and growth it offers.

To find out more or join simply visit:

earthangelsanctuary.com

(Monthly or yearly membership available)

"I believe that we will achieve peace on Earth and experience the Golden Age. My role is to awaken, inspire and support all light workers and earth angels to assist them in stepping into their power to help raise the vibration of our beautiful planet. I do that by sharing all the information I've learnt along my journey and I continue to do so..."

Sarah Rebecca Vine - aka Starlight

♥

71939356R00114

Made in the USA
Columbia, SC
08 June 2017